"Blundertail, the quest is yours,"
Lord Botolf said.

Blundertail wasn't paying the least bit of attention.

"Did you hear me?" Lord Botolf roared. "I am dubbing you a Knight of the Unrivaled and sending you on a quest to find the Goblet of Gismore! You, Blundertail. You!"

The old dinosaur turned slowly. "You want *me* to go? As a knight?"

"It is an honor fit for no other," Lord Botolf said, clearly struggling to keep his patience. "Yes, Blundertail. You."

"Ned, did you hear that?" Blundertail asked. His voice was choked with emotion. "I am to be a knight. Will you be my squire?"

"Without hesitation," Ned said. He knelt and bowed to his friend.

VISIT THE EXCITING WORLD OF

IN THESE BOOKS:

Windchaser by Scott Ciencin
River Quest by John Vornholt
Hatchling by Midori Snyder
Sabertooth Mountain by John Vornholt
Thunder Falls by Scott Ciencin
Firestorm by Gene DeWeese
The Maze by Peter David
Rescue Party by Mark A. Garland
Sky Dance by Scott Ciencin
Chomper by Donald F. Glut
Survive! by Brad Strickland
Dolphin Watch by John Vornholt

DINOTOPIA TALES OF THE TROODON KNIGHTS
Lost City by Scott Ciencin
Return to Lost City by Scott Ciencin
The Explorers by Scott Ciencin

AND COMING SOON:

Oasis by Cathy Hapka

DINOTOPIA
RETURN TO LOST CITY

by Scott Ciencin

Random House 🏠 New York

To my darling wife, Denise, for her love and inspiration;
to Alice Alfonsi for her unyielding belief and support;
to Jim Thomas for his enthusiasm and encouragement;
to Jim Gurney for his amazing creation
and the chance to once again spend time in one of my favorite places in the world;
to Michael Welply for his exciting and breathtaking covers;
and to Rose Averill and her class for providing insight
and a truly appreciated sense of wonder.

DINOTOPIA®
RETURN TO LOST CITY

CHAPTER 1

Andrew Lawton needed to talk with his brother. He had journeyed long and hard to reach Halcyon, a place that had been known for centuries as the Lost City. Now that he was here, he raced through shadowy, twisting corridors, his guide a few paces behind him.

"Slow down, Andrew," the armored Troodon said. "You never know what wonders you might miss!"

Reluctantly, Andrew obeyed. He fidgeted as his guide slowly strode up to reach him.

Andrew *had* to see Ned. It had been six months since Andrew had left his village to begin his apprenticeship as a master storyteller. His heart was heavy and his mind was fit to bursting over the final words his mentor had given him—and the difficult decision now before him. His foster brother would know what to do. Ned had always been levelheaded, and he could handle any crisis.

The Troodon walked up beside Andrew and aimed

his torch at a grand mural. In the painting, a group of saurians dressed in silly costumes danced about while fierce armored warriors looked on in stunned silence.

"The competition," Andrew said. His voice was soft. He tensed at the sight of the mural.

"Yes," the Troodon said. His name was Stonesnout and he was a great knight among the Unrivaled. "And if you look closely enough, you might see a very familiar face…"

Andrew nodded. This mural had not been here when he last visited the lost city. He drew close to it, placed his hand on the wall, and traced the outline of a single figure.

He wished he could have been surprised to see himself in the painting. Or that he could have felt excitement over the honor, but incidents like this were part of the problem that had caused him to go home and seek help.

The warrior bowed. Stonesnout was oblivious to Andrew's distress. "You performed a great service for the Unrivaled. You led us out of the shadows of our own isolation into a realm where we might help others. Such is our calling, and we had all but forgotten it. Come, there are other wonders ahead."

Andrew allowed the Troodon to lead him from one mural to another. His entire first adventure with the Unrivaled had been depicted. It began with his encounter with Arri on a moonlit road, when the lost city was thought by most to be nothing but empty ruins. As Andrew walked beside the wall, he saw a painting of the race he won against a saurian knight-in-training by "pulling an Andrew." Then he saw an image of his first meeting with Lord Botolf, the leader who had been given the name "Flopbottom" by his many detractors. All the events in which he and his friends Lian and Ned had helped the Unrivaled were depicted. The only thing the images failed to capture was how the events of those days had taught the trio so much about themselves. And, of course, they did not show all that had happened to Andrew in the months that had followed.

"I'm—I'm honored," Andrew said out of politeness and respect, though secretly he wished with all his heart that he had been spared this sight. He bowed to Stonesnout.

"*We* are honored ones," Stonesnout said. "Come. There are other wonders."

Andrew and Stonesnout walked through the corridors of outer Halcyon. When Andrew had first visited the lost city, these hallways had been strewn with discarded relics from another age. Shattered bowls and bits of armor had lain everywhere. It had been part of the city's disguise, an outer shell of decay to deter curiosity-seekers. Now they were swept and clean.

"Hold," Stonesnout said gravely. He put his torch to a brazier on his left, then lit one on his right.

Flames roared, and brilliant light erupted from crackling torches set along the walls. Lines of fire raced along vines, lighting torch after torch until the entire hallway was filled with light. The flaming vines linking the torches sagged and broke off from the assembly. They fell into little trenches of water with snakelike hisses. A scent of jasmine filled the air, and the corridor glowed golden.

"That's amazing," Andrew said.

"A wonder, yes. I *suppose*." Stonesnout shrugged. "One of Ned's inventions."

"Inventions?"

The warrior laughed again. "One of his few successful ones. Pleasing to the eye, but of little practical value. It can only be used once."

"Not really," Andrew said. "All you have to do is replace the vines."

Stonesnout stopped laughing. He narrowed his gaze as if he were deep in thought, then he cleared his throat. "Of course. You *would* be indulgent of his whims. He is your brother. Let's move on."

Andrew studied the rough, hard-set features of the knight at his side. The thirteen-year-old now had an idea of how the dinosaur had received his name.

"My teacher has always said happiness is not a state to arrive at, but simply a means of traveling," Andrew said. He spoke the words flatly, though he had done his best to put true feeling into them.

"Happiness is to do your duty well," Stonesnout

countered. "Surely *you* know this. Look ahead. There is one last wonder for you to behold."

They turned a corner, and Andrew gasped as he saw two rows of armored Troodon knights lining the golden corridor. At the end of the corridor stood a large-bellied saurian dressed in the finest armor Andrew had ever seen. It was golden and glittering. This dinosaur was an old friend.

"We have come to receive you with the honor you deserve," called Lord Botolf. "Come here, lad. I have waited months to hear another of your tales—and I can only *imagine* all you have learned as the student of a master storyteller!"

Andrew looked at his guide. Stonesnout's mouth twitched in what might have been a brief smile. Then he raised his chin and tapped Andrew on the shoulder, gently urging him forward.

Andrew was overwhelmed by the sight of so many knights in full armor. They bowed as he passed, and he nodded at each of them.

"Honor and glory," Andrew said in a small voice.

"Honor and glory!" the group answered as one in a thunderous cry.

Andrew reached Lord Botolf and dropped to one knee before the ruler of the mighty houses of the Unrivaled. Botolf hauled Andrew to his feet and hugged him tightly enough to drive the breath from Andrew's slight frame.

Botolf released him. Andrew struggled for breath

as he looked out at the assembled knights. Silverclaw, the great Troodon metalsmith, stood nearby. Strangely, Ned was not at his side!

Andrew turned swiftly. "Lord Botolf—"

Botolf stepped back and clamped a jeweled, gauntleted claw on Andrew's arm. The leader looked wistful and apologetic. "Your brother is well, have no concerns. He could not be here tonight because he is preparing a, ah, a *surprise* for you."

"Probably another contraption," Stonesnout muttered. "The surprise will be if it works!"

Lord Botolf nodded to the assembled knights. "Honor and glory. Peace be with you."

The warriors stamped their feet in unison, then bowed and dispersed. Silverclaw remained behind. He walked over to Andrew, Botolf, and Stonesnout.

"Your brother has developed some interesting new ideas," Silverclaw said. "He has used all I have taught him as a smith in some unconventional pursuits. I wish him well, but I am saddened by his absence."

"He *is* reading," Botolf said. "And that much is good. Undeniably good."

"But he spends too much time in the library around Wizenscales," Stonesnout said in a low voice that was accompanied by a growl.

"Wizenscales?" Andrew asked.

"Our antiquarian," Lord Botolf said as he led Andrew down several flights of stone stairs. "The keeper of our histories, our prized scrolls. And his name is not Wizenscales."

They came to a huge set of double doors. Botolf pushed them open.

"His name is—" Botolf began, but he stopped suddenly and gasped.

Andrew crowded in beside the ruler. Stonesnout and Silverclaw stood behind him.

"Blundertail!" Ned's voice called from within. "Look out!"

Andrew barely had time to view the vast library before disaster struck. He saw an array of glowing crystals set into the walls and hanging from the ceiling, illuminating every tiny nook and crevice. A towering ceiling arched above, painted with images of Troodon knights performing acts of chivalry. Alcoves with round storage spaces just right for holding scrolls were everywhere. Paintings, statues, and two treadmill-style scroll-readers completed the decor.

But it was what lay at the heart of the room that arrested Andrew's interest. It was unlike anything he had ever seen in any library. The long tables and couches that should have been there were gone. In their place stood a construct that was twenty-five feet high, made of wood, stone, and steel. It looked like a gigantic house of cards, with dozens of scrolls neatly packed in each triangular-shaped opening. Each scroll had a color-coded cloth tab attached to it and thin lines of wire that led down to a complex spiderweb of levers and pulleys.

An elderly Troodon in a bright crimson robe rushed past frantically, his tail whipping about. Dozens of the tiny gossamer wires had been caught by his tail, and more were becoming entangled with his every confused movement.

Ned raced toward the Troodon, waving his arms. He was even taller than when Andrew had left, and more heavily muscled. He wore a loose-fitting cream-colored shirt, a pair of simple leggings, and boots.

"Blundertail, don't move," Ned called. "Don't—"

The elderly saurian whirled, yanking even harder on the array of lines caught on his tail. "Why, Ned, what's wrong?"

That last turn was all that was needed. Andrew heard wires snap. He saw the great assembly totter and strain. And below, the massive levers ground, lifted, and snapped!

The giant scroll collector shuddered and began to tear itself apart with the strain.

"Ned, get away!" Andrew yelled.

Ned did not appear to hear Andrew. He raced toward Blundertail and attempted to free some of the wires from the saurian's tail. A heavy shadow fell on Blundertail and Ned as the contraption broke apart, and several huge pieces fell toward them!

CHAPTER 2

Stonesnout leaped into action. He snatched a ceremonial blade from the wall and raced toward Ned and Blundertail. With a single effortless swipe of the blade he cut through the wires. Dropping the weapon, he grabbed Blundertail and Ned and hauled them out of harm's way as the two-story-high scroll-keeper crumpled and fell!

"Lord Botolf, run!" Stonesnout hollered.

Andrew saw the danger. Heavy slabs of stone and metal were crashing to the floor. Some bounced high and ricocheted toward the walls. If one came toward them, it might bring serious harm—or worse.

Grabbing Lord Botolf's arm, Andrew dragged the ruler away from the double doors just as a huge section of the contraption rocketed through them and smashed into the wall. The crash was deafening, and little pieces of stone struck the pair. They bounced off Lord Botolf's armor. Andrew was left bruised and scraped.

Then a silence filled the corridor, and dust filtered out of the library.

Andrew hurried to the door. Inside, Stonesnout stood above Blundertail and Ned, both of whom looked startled but unhurt.

"Andrew Lawton," Stonesnout said, "I present you with what I hope will be your final *wonder* for the evening. If I were you, I would be wondering how many of our brave knights spent their time aiding in the construction of this worthless and costly endeavor. In fact, I would also be wondering if those same knights will now be forced to spend time away from their true studies and training to help clean up this latest in a long series of messes. It is something *I* wonder about."

Ned stood and brushed off the dirt and dust covering his leggings. "We can fix it up."

Andrew took a step closer to his brother. "I'll help Ned."

A few feet away, Blundertail wobbled to his feet.

"What happened, anyway?" Blundertail asked. "It was as if the Kraken of old had reached up through the floor and struck down our fine efforts!"

Stonesnout looked thoroughly exasperated. "Lord Botolf, with your leave?"

"Yes, brave knight," Lord Botolf said. "Take your leave."

Stonesnout stormed past Andrew and the leader of the Unrivaled. He left the room, walking away with

Silverclaw just as a group of knights arrived in response to all the noise. Botolf met them, reassuring the group that he was fine and that no one had been hurt. Then he excused himself and left Andrew alone to visit with Ned and Blundertail.

"I'm home," Andrew said. He looked at the wreckage. "How can I help?"

Ned hugged his brother, then said, "We've suffered a little setback, that's all. I can accept that there was a design flaw. I'll fix it when we reconstruct the scroll-keeper."

"I've never seen anything like this," Andrew said. "It'll be wonderful when you get it fixed up."

"I should say!" Blundertail howled. "Ned is such a clever one. All this happened because I said to him, 'If only there were a way to access the most difficult-to-reach scrolls without the use of ladders and lifts.' He devised this system so that any scroll could be brought down with a series of pulls on these levers."

The old saurian pointed at a half-crushed control center for the construct. "Many call me a foolish old dreamer, but when I look at this invention of Ned's, I don't see it as broken. Instead, I see it fully restored and working perfectly. You know what the great thinker Idlecrest says: 'Look ahead. That's where your future lies!'"

"Fine words," Andrew said. "And an even finer sentiment."

A sparkling light at the far end of the corridor

caught Andrew's attention. He pointed at it. "I think one of the crystals fell."

Ned turned and quickly counted the crystals set into the walls and hanging from the ceiling. "No, all the crystals are in place. What *is* that?"

Andrew followed Ned and Blundertail to the source of the light. One of the pieces of Ned's construct had smashed into the wall and shattered a section of shelving. Beyond lay a small room with a single glowing light.

"A hidden room?" Blundertail said. "Impossible!"

"Very possible," Andrew said. He peered through the opening. "It's loaded with scrolls!"

Ned and Andrew worked to make the opening wide enough for Blundertail to fit through, but they did not have the saurian's strength.

Blundertail turned to the pair. "I can excavate this room and catalog every scroll within it by morning. You know it's what I live for. That and a good joust!"

Ned leaped forward, pretending to carry a lance. Blundertail did the same. They rushed at each other. Ned pretended that he had been knocked down by the elderly Troodon's imaginary lance.

"I cannot beat you, glorious knight," Ned laughed.

"That is why you are the squire and I am the knight," Blundertail said. "At least in my dreams."

Andrew was fascinated by the elderly Troodon, and a part of him wanted to hear more about Blundertail's life and dreams. Another part of him wanted nothing more to do with history. He was a storyteller, after all.

The words of his mentor, Talltail, came to him: *It is only by learning what is and what was that we can make up tales of what might have been and what may be still.*

"You want to be a knight?" Andrew asked.

Blundertail sighed. He gestured at the precious scrolls strewn around the library. "I have lived all these adventures by reading. But to actually live one, as you did, ah, that would be the fulfillment of all my dreams!"

"If only it were so," Ned said, rubbing his hand on the elderly Troodon's back.

"Enough!" Blundertail said. "I have work to do, and the two of you need time together." He raised his chin as Stonesnout might. "Begone, my squire, and my squire's brother. I shall be here in the morning, and we shall work on the great scroll-keeper then!"

Andrew and Ned bowed, then ran off happily.

CHAPTER 3

It took hours for Andrew and Ned to get clear of the lost city. Andrew was approached constantly by Troodon knights who wished to thank him for all he had done or ask him to visit their houses. When Andrew said he wanted to sleep in his old bed in the village, one of the warriors insisted on providing transportation.

They were led outside Halcyon's gates to a small barn where a half-dozen former Copro Carts were kept. The strong knight who had offered to take them home swiftly was named Thundersnout. He donned a harness attached to the spotless and sweet-smelling cart and gestured for Andrew and Ned to get in.

"This is quite an honor," Thundersnout said. "The inventor of the shawrick—"

"Rickshaw," Ned said quickly. "And I didn't invent it. I just took the idea from something my friend Lian told me existed in her native land."

"So modest," Thundersnout said. "An inventor

and the liberator of Halcyon in my humble presence. I am glad."

"Liberator?" Andrew asked as he climbed into the rickshaw with Ned. "I'm just a storyteller."

"Both brothers are modest," Thundersnout said. "You must regale me with the tale of how your stories liberated our minds and led us back into the light of outer Dinotopia."

Andrew winced. "That's not really a story. That's something that actually happened."

"It is a glorious tale," Thundersnout said. "It is told everywhere on the island. I know. I have traveled far in the last several months. I have returned only to gather my family and bring them with me when I leave again!"

They set out from the barn slowly and carefully, but once they were on the road, the Troodon's powerful legs quickly brought them to a surprising speed. Andrew couldn't have dreamed of running so quickly.

"Well?" Ned asked as they bumped and bounced in the cart. "Tell the tale."

"It's not a tale," Andrew said. Then he settled back and stared at the stars. "But I'll tell it anyway…"

He told the shortest version of his history with the Troodons that he had yet been able to devise. He finished just as Thundersnout brought them into the village, to the door of their father's inn.

A tear of joy shone in the knight's eye as he thanked them both and bid them farewell.

Andrew looked around nervously.

"What's wrong?" Ned asked. "Are you worried about having to deal with more of your adoring public?"

In truth, that was exactly what Andrew was worried about.

"Well, don't," Ned said. "We'll climb up the back and sneak into our room, if that would make you feel better. Though I have to admit I'm a little confused. I thought you lived to tell tales."

"Stories, yes," Andrew said. "Tales. There's a difference between a made-up story and something that really happened."

"I see," Ned said with a grin. "You're a prisoner of your own fame. Everywhere you go, you are known and recognized, and since that is exactly what you hoped and dreamed would one day happen, it is a terrible thing."

"Can we just climb?" Andrew asked.

Ned led him around to the rear of the Dragon's Snout Inn and they climbed up to the bedroom they'd shared for years. The window was open, but the sill was filled with scrolls and half-finished bits of metal sculpture. Ned moved them, then helped his brother inside. Andrew almost tripped on all the clutter on the floor.

"What have you done with this place?" Andrew asked. "Turned it into your inventor's lair?"

Ned lit a lamp with amber panes. "Exactly."

As light filled the room, Andrew was stunned to see scrolls with designs for contraptions of every type. Models and prototypes of little devices lined the walls, the floor, and even the ceiling. The mattress from his bed had been rolled up and stuffed in a corner, and the bedframe had been used as storage space. Ned gently cleared the area, and Andrew helped him spread the mattress back on the frame.

While Ned snuck downstairs to get some food for them from the kitchen, Andrew looked through the many odd designs Ned had dreamed up. Some were very practical, like mechanical lifters to help humans or saurians who were injured or disabled to move things about. Others were fantastic, like flying machines and moving roads!

Ned returned and handed Andrew a bowl of soup and a plate of his favorite breads and fruits.

"Don't worry," Ned said. "I didn't mention to anyone that you're here. You're safe for the night from your admirers."

Andrew nodded. Ned thought this was a jest on Andrew's part. But it was truly the major reason he had come home so soon.

They ate in silence until Andrew said, "I need your advice."

"Sure," Ned said. He lay back on his own bunk, setting his plates aside. "First, though, I want to thank you."

"For what?"

"Andrew, do you remember the last words you spoke to me before you left?"

He did. "'It's time to start living the life we've imagined.'"

"You were so full of hope and happiness—it was an inspiration to me. I loved the way of the smith. I felt I was learning so much with Silverclaw. But I also felt there was something more."

"What do you mean?" Andrew asked.

"I felt as if something was missing in my life," Ned said. "Silverclaw seemed to sense my restlessness. He urged me to visit the library, to read the scrolls of others who had walked the path of the smith. I thought it was a wonderful idea—that I would find what I thought was missing."

Andrew smiled at the thought of Ned spending hours poring over scrolls. His foster brother had changed so much since he had arrived on the island as a proud, boastful dolphinback. He was humble and earnest now, though as driven as ever to succeed.

"I didn't just read scrolls about smiths," Ned said. "I read about the history of the Unrivaled. I learned so much, especially from the teachings of Idlecrest."

"Really?" Andrew asked.

"It's pretty simple, really," Ned said. "You're always talking about the power of words. They convey thoughts. And as we've been taught, we are what we think. All that we are arises from our thoughts. With our thoughts, we make the world."

"I've read those words," Andrew said. "They're from Idlecrest's 'Diversity: The Art of Thinking Independently Together.'"

Ned smiled. He looked at the ceiling and yawned. He couldn't help himself. It had been a tiring day for both of them.

"'The great use of life is to spend it on something that will outlast us,'" Ned said, quoting the philosopher. "I plan to build something monumental. I'm going to use the skills Silverclaw taught me to create something that will help me to be remembered."

"But a kind word, a loving gesture, a bit of help when it's most needed—that can outlast and outweigh any monument," Andrew said.

"Maybe," Ned said. "But not everyone has that to give. This is my special talent, just as storytelling is yours. You should be happy for me."

Andrew nodded. "I am. But I really do need to talk to you."

Settling on his bed, Ned picked up his pillow and rested it on his forehead, partially shielding his eyes from the light.

"So talk," Ned said. "You have my complete attention."

Ned yawned again.

Looking away, Andrew focused his attention on the lantern's flickering glow. He felt too ashamed to look at his brother while he said what he needed to.

"My days with Talltail haven't been what I expected," Andrew said. "You've seen it. I'm recognized everywhere I go. And while it's wonderful that people want to hear what I have to say, they have no real interest in any of the adventures I've dreamed up. All they want is for me to recount our adventure in Halcyon with the Unrivaled."

Ned said something, but it was low and mumbled. Andrew went on.

"My audience will listen when I tell a made-up story, but only out of politeness. They don't respond the way I've seen them act when any other storyteller tells the exact same story. They are only waiting, hoping I'll get to the historical recounting of what happened to us and the Troodons. Then they become interested. Then they laugh and cheer, and only then can I get anything out of them. It's frustrating."

Andrew thought of the final words he had shared with his mentor.

"Talltail told me I've disappointed him," Andrew said. "He says I've become full of myself. 'You've gone from being in love with the stories you tell to being in love with the sound of your own words. That is not fitting for a master storyteller. Travel home, travel where you will these next few months. But return to me only if storytelling is your one true joy.' Those were his words. But he doesn't understand. How can I be a storyteller when I'm also the story?"

Andrew waited for Ned to say something.

And waited.

Finally, he heard soft snoring coming from the bed next to him. Andrew looked over and saw that Ned was sound asleep. He doubted that his brother had heard a word he said.

Andrew rose, put out the lantern, and found his way back to bed.

He stared at the ceiling in the dim moonlight for hours before he drifted off to sleep.

CHAPTER 4

Ned shook Andrew awake before dawn. "We have to get back to Halcyon. I know Blundertail will be beside himself waiting to tell us about those new scrolls!"

Andrew was groggy from getting so little sleep, but he immediately pictured the homecoming that would be waiting for him. And as much as he wanted to see his parents—and Lian—he knew that telling the tale of the lost city would be an inevitable duty thrust on him in the course of the day. So he roused himself and followed Ned out the window.

They were clear of the village and on the road as the sun rose. It was a gorgeous sight. Blinding yellow-white rays broke over the horizon.

Ned had packed a bag filled with breads, fruits, and teas that he had steeped, then chilled. Delicious!

It took hours for them to reach Halcyon on foot. At least Ned had found a shortcut through a mountain pass that had cut down the length of their journey. Too bad they hadn't known about the pass the very first time they had walked from the village to Halcyon.

Andrew wondered if he should put it in the tale the next time he told it. A shortcut was found through the mountains...

Ned regaled Andrew with tales of the wonders he planned to unleash upon Dinotopia. Andrew tried several times to bring up his own dilemma, but Ned was so enthusiastic and hopeful that he finally gave up. There would be time for them to have a proper talk later. Andrew was sure of it.

They found Blundertail inside the hidden room of the library. The old saurian turned as they tapped on the wall, sweeping his tail across a shelf filled with glass bottles. Andrew moved quickly, catching all but one before it struck the floor and shattered.

"Oh," Blundertail said. "I wonder what made it fall?"

Andrew bent down. He pointed at the seal on the scroll that had been placed in the bottle. It showed a human and a saurian shielding their eyes from the sun while looking out together over a rock. "Well, isn't that something? I *recognize* that mark. My mentor, Talltail, told me that is the sign of the Explorers Club."

The Troodon turned so quickly that Ned had to leap out of the way of his tail, which sailed right past his stomach.

"The Explorers Club!" Blundertail said. "They

were members of the Unrivaled. Some of the most valiant and most beloved knights who ever lived!"

Andrew pointed at the human figure on the seal. "Well, the group was *started* by the Unrivaled, but it was open to anyone."

"Yes, yes," Blundertail said. "It must be so. I have a limited number of historical records here, you see. Not like what one might find in Waterfall City."

Andrew opened the scroll, and Blundertail bent over swiftly to read it. Ned had to leap out of the way again, but he didn't complain. He crouched next to the saurian, and they skimmed the text together.

"This is a tale of their final adventure!" Blundertail said. "A historical record of their search for the Goblet of Gismore!"

The Troodon flopped back and landed hard on the floor. His clawed hands twitched excitedly.

Ned took the scroll from Andrew.

"This tells where they found the goblet and what they did with it before disbanding!" Ned said.

Andrew shrugged. "Well—there are many such scrolls. Many versions of the tale."

"This one has the seal!" Ned insisted.

"Yes," Andrew said. "A very nice touch on the storyteller's part. I've seen it done with other scrolls."

Ned shook his head. "This is real."

"No argument," Andrew said. He was very excited as he looked around the room. "An entire treasure room of new tales to tell."

Blundertail cleared his throat. "Young Andrew, you do not understand. You *have* heard the tale of the Kraken, the sea monster that once swam in the waters underground where we fish for food."

Of course he had. It was part of his story.

"Such tales only exist because they have been passed down as spoken word," Blundertail said. "They are written on no scrolls in this library. Oh, there is a scroll that contains an accout of a Liopleurodon sighting, and anyone may read it and wonder if the legend of the Kraken started there. But there are no fanciful tales in this library. They were removed at the request of Lord Balhamous centuries ago."

"Maybe that's why this room was sealed up," Andrew said. "To preserve these stories for a later time—"

Ned turned quickly. "Andrew, *what* is your problem? Blundertail explained that this has to be a historical record. It has the seal. What else do you want?"

To read these stories, Andrew thought. *To be the one who brings them to the light of outer Dinotopia. Then maybe the audience will be more interested in the tales I have to tell than in me and what I went through. Maybe with* these *I could be a real storyteller again.*

"Aren't there scrolls about the Great Dragon of the Outer Dark?" Andrew asked. "I've heard that story told many times in Halcyon."

"Not a single scroll," Blundertail said. "Which is

not to say it didn't happen. There are gaps in many of the historical records."

"Wait," Andrew said. "The dragon is real but the Kraken is not? The dragon might have been a Quetzalcoatlus. A Skybax with a forty-foot wingspan."

"Or it may be something that flew away and hasn't yet returned to Dinotopia," Blundertail said mildly. "Think of Grokle, who travels with Maxim's Cavalcade of Wonders. A saurian with a crocodilian head? A year ago, we might have thought the suggestion fanciful. A mere story. But there he is, scales and all."

"Come on," Ned whispered. "It's a historical document. Forget it."

Andrew shook his head. "That seal could be duplicated very easily. I'm sorry. I think what you're looking at is a story. A made-up tale."

Blundertail sniffed. Andrew followed suit without thinking. The air was very stale.

"This room *has* been sealed for centuries," Blundertail said. "Imagine the other wonders these scrolls must hold. Their historical significance cannot be underestimated!"

"As *stories,* I agree," Andrew said.

Ned held the scroll close to Blundertail. "This *is* real, isn't it? Real in a way you can prove?"

The old Troodon touched his claw to the broken seal. Then he brought it to his tongue. "Yes! The Explorers Club used a wax that was peppered with a smattering of herbs. The exact blend is known only to the Unrivaled. This seal was made from such wax."

Ned nodded excitedly. "That proves it, then!"

"No," Andrew said. "It only proves that a member of the Unrivaled created the story. I have no doubt of that, considering the use of language and where it's been found."

"There's only one thing to do," Ned said.

Blundertail rose on wobbly legs. He turned sharply, knocking over some more jars. They broke, and he turned again, smashing a few more.

"What keeps causing that?" Blundertail asked. "Are we experiencing another earthquake?"

Ned patted the old dinosaur on the back. "That kind of thing happens here a lot, it's true. Isn't that right, Andrew?"

Andrew put up his hands. "Yes. *That's* true."

"We must arrange an audience with Lord Botolf!" Blundertail said. "The great Goblet of Gismore is said to possess the power to bring harmony to all who hold it. Such an artifact must be delivered into the hands of all Dinotopians."

Taking the scroll from Ned, Andrew read it through to the end. "It says here they *buried* the goblet. And afterward, they saw no further point to exploring and went their separate ways. The members of the Explorers Club were known for their wisdom. Even if this were something more than a story, shouldn't we respect their wishes and leave the goblet where they put it?"

"No," Ned said quickly. "Maybe once they had what they wanted from it, they didn't think about anyone else."

"That would have been most unchivalrous," Blundertail muttered.

"I could think of a million other reasons," Ned said. "Maybe they *meant* to tell others about it, and that's why this was written. What's important is what we do with the information."

Blundertail nodded. "To quote from the great scrolls of Idlecrest, 'It is not in the stars to hold our destiny, but in ourselves.'"

Andrew cocked his head to one side. "That wasn't Idlecrest. William Shakespeare—"

Ned cleared his throat. Andrew looked over to see the wizened Troodon staring at him with a confused and crestfallen expression.

"Oh, no," Andrew added quickly. "I was wrong. That was Idlecrest after all. Shakespeare said something similar, that's all."

"He probably read Idlecrest's scrolls!" Ned said.

Andrew nodded. "Probably."

Blundertail straightened his robe. "Then our path is clear. We must convince Lord Botolf that a party must be sent. The Goblet of Gismore must be retrieved!"

CHAPTER 5

Andrew walked quietly behind Ned and Blundertail. They were busy speculating on who Lord Botolf might send on such an important quest. Certainly Stonesnout. He was the greatest of Halcyon's knights. Just last month, he had rescued three saurians from certain disaster when a fire broke out in a nearby forest. His courage was unmatched.

"Arri and Na'dra would leap at the chance," Ned said. "But who knows where they are or what adventures they're having right now."

Andrew noted that Ned sounded a little wistful. Just like Blundertail.

"Ah, to be young and to go adventuring," Blundertail said. His shoulders sagged. "I wonder what that's like? The adventuring part, I mean."

"You were never a knight?" Andrew asked. Ned drew back, and Andrew narrowly avoided an elbow in the ribs. "Well, I mean—Halcyon was closed off for centuries! How could anyone have gone adventuring? What was I thinking?"

"I'm sure I don't know," Ned said.

Andrew caught the frown his brother shot at him.

"Well, yes, that was part of it," Blundertail said. "But I have always had a gift for caring for scrolls. I love them so!"

"And you, as a storyteller, should appreciate that," Ned said.

Andrew nodded. His brother was right.

As they walked through the corridors of the lost city, Blundertail spread his tiny arms. "Ah, to race through the open fields, the sun on my face, a great quest before me…" He sighed. "It's something I've always dreamed of doing. But it is a thing for the young. And I was never any good with all the skills needed to be a knight, try as I might."

Blundertail stumbled into a knight who was turning a corner, knocking a collection of plates from his hands. They fell in a tangled mess. The knight shoved Blundertail away from him and griped under his breath as he picked up the dented steel plates and went on his way.

"Really," Andrew said. "Not cut out to be a knight. I never would have thought that."

This time, Andrew *wasn't* quick enough to avoid Ned's elbow.

They arrived at the opulent outer chambers of Lord Botolf's receiving rooms and were forced to wait nearly an hour before a squire opened the doors and ushered them inside.

Stonesnout stood beside Botolf's throne. "Lord Botolf, should I check to see if there is anything breakable within range?"

The portly Troodon gave the knight a warning glance. He gestured for the trio to come forward.

Blundertail clutched the scroll. Ned took it from him and unrolled it for Lord Botolf.

Andrew tried to conceal his nervousness as he looked around to see if anything breakable was indeed within range. He stood back as Blundertail and Ned told the story and made their urgent request that a party made up of Halcyon's finest warriors be sent to retrieve the legendary goblet. At one point, he caught Stonesnout staring at him, the saurian knight's chin lifted high. Was Stonesnout studying him? Why?

Andrew believed he could guess. Stonesnout had treated Andrew as an equal when the lad had first returned. The knight's good opinion of Andrew clearly had lessened since then—and being involved in this silly business wouldn't help matters.

A sudden pressure on his arm made Andrew turn. Ned stood beside him.

"Lord Botolf is speaking to you," Ned said.

Andrew bowed apologetically. "Forgive me, Lord Botolf."

"Lost in another of your fine stories, were you?" Lord Botolf asked.

Andrew scrambled to think of an appropriate reply. "I hope it'll turn out to be a fine one."

"Tell it to me when you're done," Lord Botolf said. "For now, what is your opinion on all of this? Do you think a party should be sent to look for the goblet?"

Andrew looked at Blundertail, who was standing off to one side, studying an array of blunted swords. The old saurian pretended to have one of the weapons in his claw. He thrust, parried, and leaped back, nearly toppling from his feet.

Ned stared at Andrew with an urgent plea in his eyes. Andrew glanced away and met Stonesnout's hard and penetrating gaze.

Andrew sighed. "No. I honestly think it would be a waste of time. These are stories, not historical records. I'd like to read them. I think they should be shared with others, but in the proper way—as tales to inspire and lessons to be learned."

He heard Ned hiss in frustration. Then he saw Blundertail spin in surprise—sweeping the entire collection of swords from their holders and scattering them across the floor!

Blundertail jumped at the noise and looked down in surprise. "The earthquakes touch even here!" Then the librarian looked back to Lord Botolf. "I'm so sorry—I was thinking of the tale of Ripclaw the Mighty and the day he faced the Great Dragon of the Outer Dark! Well, who will be sent?"

Lord Botolf sighed. "I am still considering the matter."

Blundertail happily took Ned's arm. "This is *such* an exciting day!"

Andrew followed as they left Lord Botolf's chamber. Midway down the hall, Ned spun toward Andrew.

"Thanks for all your help!" Ned said.

"What did you want me to say?" Andrew asked. "I told Lord Botolf what I honestly believe. Was I supposed to make up a story?"

"Stories are wonderful," Blundertail said absently.

Ned frowned and looked back. "We'll talk another time."

"Sounds like a good idea."

Andrew watched as Ned led Blundertail back to the library. He leaned against the wall. A mural depicting a brave Troodon knight performing a heroic rescue in the outer realms of Dinotopia captured his attention. The knight stood between a tiny two-foot-high Hypsilophodon and an angry young Tyrannosaurus in the Rainy Basin. The knight held his shield high and his sword low. Andrew knew from his reading that a knight could drive a juvenile Tyrannosaurus off with a few tiny nicks and a fierce attitude.

What had he done to his friends? And why wasn't he at least open to the idea that the goblet might be real and could be found? Goodness knew, he could use a little harmony.

He looked at the painting again and thought of Stonesnout's commanding gaze.

It wouldn't be right to send a brave and capable knight like Arri or Na'dra or Stonesnout after the goblet, Andrew thought. He brightened inwardly as an idea formed in his mind. *But who says it has to be a great knight who goes on the quest?*

He hurried back to Lord Botolf's chambers. The doors were ajar, and he heard voices.

Andrew was about to knock when he recognized Stonesnout's voice—and heard what the knight was saying.

"He's a one-dinosaur disaster area," Stonesnout snarled. "What more can be said about him?"

"Blundertail has his virtues," Lord Botolf said. "He is loyal and kind. And he loves our history. He is the best versed of us all in the ancient histories and the First Code of Chivalry."

Andrew drew closer to the door. He knew it was wrong to eavesdrop, but he sensed that important events were unfolding.

"Deeds, not words, define the individual," Stonesnout continued. "Blundertail's deeds define him as a menace and a disgrace."

"You go too far," Lord Botolf said.

"I doubt that I go far enough," Stonesnout said. "'Not only must we be good, we must be good for something.'"

"You quote from the First Code," Lord Botolf

said. "Have a care. Words like those can circle around and come back to the one who casually tosses them about."

Stonesnout growled. "All I'm saying is this: Sending a true knight of the Unrivaled on such a task is a waste of valuable resources. So why not send Blundertail instead? At least he won't be *here* to break anything!"

Andrew crept even closer to the door. He peeked inside the room and saw Lord Botolf looking away in deep contemplation.

Stonesnout stepped into the shadows behind Lord Botolf's enormous and ornate throne, smirking.

Andrew felt chilled. This was a *joke* to Stonesnout. He would laugh with the other knights who shared his point of view as poor Blundertail was sent off on his "great quest."

That wasn't what Andrew wanted. He *was* going to suggest sending Blundertail, yes, but only because it might do the old dinosaur some good to live out an adventure—or at least to get out of that musty library and see the rest of the island. But now—

A voice from behind Andrew startled him. It was Ned's voice, and he sounded distressed!

"Blundertail, your robe, your feet are caught in your—"

Andrew turned just in time to see a blur of gray, green, and purple flying at him. Blundertail crashed into him, and they both smashed against the door and tumbled into Lord Botolf's chamber.

Rolling away, Andrew saw Ned rush in and help Blundertail to his feet. The wobbly dinosaur turned suddenly and shattered a collection of crystal statues near the door. He stumbled ahead, clearly surprised by the sound, and flopped about until he flung himself right into Lord Botolf's ample lap!

"These earthquakes and tremors!" Blundertail cried. "When will they cease?"

Stonesnout dragged Blundertail away from Lord Botolf. The elderly Troodon's claws accidentally tore Botolf's fine crimson and black robes.

"Oh, goodness, I must get those trimmed," Blundertail muttered.

Andrew stepped forward. "Lord Botolf, if I could just—"

Lord Botolf raised a single claw, calling for silence. Blundertail walked in circles, muttering to himself. "Odd, no cracks in the floor, yet the tremors were so severe!"

"The quest is yours," Lord Botolf said.

Andrew watched his brother's face light up with delight.

Blundertail wasn't paying the least bit of attention.

"Did you hear me, Blundertail?" Lord Botolf roared. "I am dubbing you a Knight of the Unrivaled and sending you on a quest to find the Goblet of Gismore! You, Blundertail. You!"

The old dinosaur turned slowly. "You want *me* to go? As a knight?"

"It is an honor fit for no other," Lord Botolf said. He looked frustrated and pushed beyond his limits. "Yes, Blundertail. You."

"Ned, did you hear that?" Blundertail asked. His voice was choked with emotion. "I am to be a knight. Will you be my squire?"

"Without hesitation," Ned said. He knelt and bowed to his friend.

Stonesnout surged forward, alarmed. "Lord Botolf, I can see the wisdom of sending Wizenscales here on his *quest*, but surely not as a *knight!*"

"Remember what I said about words coming back to you in ways you do not expect," Lord Botolf said. "Consider that the next time you choose to open your maw. Now go, all of you!"

Ned led Blundertail from the chamber. The young inventor whooped and hollered in victory. Stonesnout stalked off angrily. Andrew knew he should follow, but he couldn't bring himself to go. He had to try to fix things while there was still a chance.

"What?" Lord Botolf snapped.

"Lord Botolf, I don't think it's wise to send Blundertail and Ned off alone," Andrew said. "Do you?"

"If you're really that concerned, I give you leave to go with them. In fact, take with you all who are foolish enough to believe in such wild tales!"

Andrew was startled. "It was a 'wild tale' I spun that kept you in power."

Lord Botolf sat back on his throne. "Out of friendship, I will forget you said that. Now leave. I have said all I have to say on this subject."

Andrew bowed, then left the chamber, his heart heavy, his thoughts a whirlwind.

CHAPTER 6

Andrew left Halcyon and returned alone to his village. He was comforted by how little things had changed. His mother and father were overjoyed to see him, and he entertained humans and saurians for hours with the tale of his first adventure in the lost city. He thought about telling them the new story of the Explorers Club, but he could no longer view that tale with the same excitement.

A storyteller must never seem gloomy or preoccupied, Talltail had told him often enough. *If you must, tell a story that you could tell in your sleep. But do it well, and don't let on to the crowd that you're not putting your heart into your performance. Do that, and soon you will hear their laughter, feel their tension, and your gloom will lift and your preoccupation vanish. You will be in the moment, and even you will be entertained by this story you have told so many times!*

Andrew tried, but he could not follow his mentor's advice. He was glad when the tale was done.

"I have another story," Andrew said to the already dispersing crowd. "It's about an Apatosaurus who misplaced his shadow!"

"Another time," a young mother said.

"We wouldn't want to tax you," a towering Spinosaurus said.

"I've heard that one," a little boy added.

And soon Andrew was done. He entered his father's inn and sat down with the burly man in the taproom.

"The Dragon's Snout Inn hasn't been the same since you left," his father said.

"You miss me that much?" Andrew asked brightly.

"No, that's not it!" his father said. "Well, of course we miss you. It's just that we've never been so busy. Humans and saurians travel from all over the island to visit Halcyon and to see our sketches of you when you were young. We've had to bring in extra help. You've caught us at a slow time."

Andrew could barely hear his father over all the humans and saurians speaking in the crowded room. And he was very much aware that people were staring at him and pointing while his mother served sweet fruits to one and all.

But the person he most wanted to see wasn't there.

"Where's Lian?" Andrew asked his father.

His dad looked away. "She's—staying with friends."

"I thought she was going to learn to be one with the earth," Andrew said. "She wrote to me and told me how excited she was to learn the ways of farming!"

"Yes," his father said. "She *was* excited..." He let out a low, deep breath. "Perhaps you should see her. She asked not to be bothered, but she had to know you were coming. I'll take you to her myself."

His father led him to the outskirts of the village, to a forest filled with hundred-foot-tall metasequoias. He nodded upward. "She's there."

Andrew covered his eyes to shield them from the glare of the midday sun. About midway up the tree, he saw a little house that reminded him of a dwelling in Treetown.

"That wasn't here when I left," Andrew said.

"She spent two months building it. Just finished yesterday, so I understand."

"I thought you said she was staying with friends," Andrew said.

A caw sounded from above. Andrew was surprised to see a flock of Archaeopteryx circling above.

"*Those* are her friends," Andrew's father said. "She likes them because they can't talk back."

Andrew ran his hand through his hair. Another complication lay before him. Still, who better to give him advice than Lian? He loved his father very much, but Lian understood him better than he understood himself. It was one of her many gifts.

Andrew noticed a small bare patch of ground a few feet away. He thought of Lian's beautiful garden back home. This patch of land was about the same size, and little rocks surrounded it, yet nothing grew within its borders. In fact, it looked as if it had been tilled until it would never bear seedlings again.

"I'm going up," Andrew said.

"Be careful," his father replied. "It can be tricky up there."

Andrew nodded, sensing that his father was talking about more than just the climb. As he made his way up the tree, shinnying from one branch to another, he saw a shadow moving just above him.

"Lian!" he called.

The dark figure didn't answer. Finally, Andrew reached the little tree house he had spied from below. Two of the rainbow-colored Archaeopteryx stepped on what might have been a bedroll, shredding it with their claws.

"Shoo! Shoo!" Andrew said, waving his hands and advancing purposefully to drive them off. "Get away from there."

"*You* get away," a voice said from above.

Andrew was only vaguely aware as a figure descended from above, grabbed his hair, and yanked him backward.

With a cry of surprise, Andrew flopped onto his back! The pair of Archaeopteryx cawed defiantly and continued to shred the bedroll.

A lithe figure dropped from above. She had silken raven hair, a heart-shaped face, and jade green eyes. She wore a black kimono and she was barefoot.

Lian.

"Oh," Lian said. "It's you." She frowned, staring into his eyes. "And you need something."

Andrew gestured at the Archaeopteryx. "They were tearing up your bedroll."

"I don't have a bedroll. I sleep on the floor. *That's* their toy."

"Oh," Andrew said. He sat down and crossed his legs. He had expected Lian to greet him with a hug and a kind word. What had happened to her since he left?

Lian sat cross-legged before him. "What do you need?"

He watched her cool, beautiful features, surprised by their hardness. There was something strange about the way she held herself, her back rigid and her shoulders tight. She made him think of Stonesnout.

Andrew told the tale of his return to Halcyon and his misadventure with Ned and Blundertail. When he finished, Lian raised a single eyebrow.

"So you're wondering if you should go with them," Lian said. "If, in my opinion, you should."

"Um, actually—"

"Yes, go. Now good-bye." She stood and walked over to the Archaeopteryx. One of them let her scratch his neck.

"It's more complicated than that!" Andrew protested.

Lian shrugged. "Only if you make it that way."

"Stonesnout thinks—"

"You already told me what he thinks," Lian said. "I find it unfortunate."

"I do, too," Andrew said. "Blundertail is very kind. He doesn't deserve—"

"No," Lian said. "I think it's unfortunate if you truly have become the kind of person who cares so much about what others think. The Andrew I knew and loved would be at home packing a bag right now to go join his friends."

"I just don't want to see them be disappointed," Andrew said. "I know what that's like."

"We all do. But I have a feeling there's something more to your reservations."

Andrew was silent. He waited. Finally, he said, "You won't help."

"Of course I'll help," Lian said. "I'll come with you."

"To speak with Ned?" Andrew asked hopefully.

For the first time, Lian smiled. "No, silly. To look for the goblet."

CHAPTER 7

At dusk, Andrew stood on the road leading east from Halcyon. Ned and Blundertail were just setting out. Andrew could see their tiny figures in the distance, the Troodon knight and his squire departing from the partially restored front gates of the lost city. A group of knights hailed them and waved banners in the air as they passed. Many cheered. Only Stonesnout stood back and kept his claws motionless.

Blundertail trundled toward Andrew, clanking and clattering. He wore the most ancient, shabbily put together suit of armor Andrew had ever seen.

Beside Blundertail, Ned was beaming. He looked at his friend with undisguised pride.

"I told you they would like your armor once we were through with it," Ned said. "Each piece is an authentic relic. No one has worn this armor in more than a century."

"It is indeed an honor," Blundertail said, "if a bit

cumbersome. I'm not certain I can move with my natural grace in this!"

"You'll be fine," Ned said. "I have no worries."

Ned's smile faded when he saw Andrew waiting. He rushed ahead of Blundertail and reached Andrew as quickly as the heavy satchels he carried would allow.

"You're carrying bags," Ned said, pointing at what Andrew held. "We've already got all the supplies and gifts we can carry."

Andrew simply smiled. He understood that Ned was trying to ask him to stay behind. "I think I need an adventure, too. I'm coming with you."

Ned stared at him in disbelief. "You're—oh no you're not!"

A few clanks and crashes later, Blundertail stood beside them. "Young Andrew! Come to entertain us with a tale before we depart?"

"Right," Ned said quickly. "But we really don't have time—"

"I'll walk with you," Andrew offered. "That way I can tell my story while we go. It's about the Explorers Club. One I heard in my travels. I don't know if it's just a made-up story or if it might be a historical document. I do know it came from a scroll. I thought maybe you could tell me your thoughts after you've heard it."

"Yes, of course!" Blundertail cried.

Ned threw up his hands in defeat. "All right."

They walked down the road. Andrew looked back, wondering where Lian was. She knew when the group was leaving. Had she changed her mind about joining them?

True, she had seemed a little distant, but he had missed her for so long and hoped for her company. Besides, she would come back to her old self in time. He knew it!

"Whoa!" Andrew cried as he tripped on a rock that had fallen into the road. He stumbled but did not fall.

"I guess you should be watching where you're going," Ned said.

"And slow down," Blundertail urged. "The great philosopher Idlecrest says progress has little to do with speed but much to do with direction!"

Andrew smiled. Talltail had said something similar.

The stars appeared as they walked. Streaks of amber and crimson carved themselves upon the horizon as the sunlight faded.

"Tell us the story!" Blundertail said brightly. "I do hope it has action and adventure!"

"All that and more," Andrew said. "It's a tale of the Great Dragon of the Outer Dark."

"Oh, no, it *can't* be," Blundertail said. "The dragon was vanquished long before the Explorers Club was formed. This must be a story, not a historical document. How sad."

"Not necessarily," Andrew said. "The way I heard it, the dragon was only *thought* to be vanquished."

Andrew looked around and wondered if Ned and Blundertail intended to *walk* the entire distance to the Rocky Pass. That couldn't be their plan—could it?

Then he realized that he might have been foolish to think they even had a plan. After all, knights traditionally relied on their wits, skill, and good fortune. And Blundertail was now a Knight of the Unrivaled!

They walked along Mudnest Trail as the golden glow in the distance dwindled even more.

"It began with a song," Andrew said. "A simple song sung with such passion that it might have made the great stones of the Backbone Mountains dance with delight. Instead, it woke a sleeping dragon."

"Who sang the song?" asked Blundertail. "I don't recall any of the members of the Explorers Club being great bards."

"It wasn't one of them who sang it," Andrew explained. He shifted the heavy bags he carried over his shoulder. "In those days, long before the Explorers Club found the Goblet of Gismore, the group was made up of just five brave Troodon knights. No humans had yet joined their number."

"I know them!" Blundertail shouted. "I know them all so well I can practically see their faces on the clouds crossing the moon above."

"Then tell Ned about them," Andrew said. He noticed that Ned had been searching through one of his bags, trying to find something.

"Oh, yes!" Blundertail said. "Ned, the Explorers Club was a place for those with a sense of wonder in their hearts. Those who were dreamers *and* doers."

Ned looked up and grinned. "Like us. First you dream, then you make the dream a reality."

"Yes!" Blundertail said. "There was Pointynog, who was *quite* clever. Always at his side was Snicknik, who was rumored to be the speediest knight who ever lived. While Pointynog liked to think things through, Snicknik believed in leaping in crest-first!"

Andrew grinned. Blundertail seemed so happy. Maybe Lian was right. Who cared what Stonesnout thought? Blundertail was having an adventure!

"There were three more," Blundertail said. "Hardshell, who was the strongest the Unrivaled had ever known, Seeno, the stealthiest, and Plodnob, the most jovial!"

Andrew watched Ned yank a pair of goggles with an odd contraption welded to its side from his bag. Only when a golden light emerged did Andrew realize that a lantern had been added to the goggles.

"This will make it easier for us to see," Ned said.

The light shone directly ahead, yet Ned stumbled and weaved as they walked. Blundertail followed Ned's movements precisely, but Andrew hung back.

Ned's contraption is lighting the way ahead, but it's blinding him at the same time, Andrew realized.

"You must make one of those for me!" Blundertail

called. He tapped his rickety headpiece. "You could weld it right on!"

Ned laughed with pride, then fell into a ditch. There was a crash, and the light was extinguished. Andrew and Blundertail reached him quickly. Ned sat in the ditch, staring at his broken goggles.

"Just a little design flaw," Ned said. "I can fix it."

"I'm sure you can," Blundertail agreed.

"I'll be right back," Andrew said. He left Ned and Blundertail talking and walked into the nearby woods. It didn't take him long to find a heavy branch, leaves, a vine, and some flint. He fashioned a torch, lit it, and went back to the others.

"The story," Blundertail said. "You must tell us what happens!"

The pair were on their feet, walking in the wrong direction. Andrew nodded and took the lead, gently urging Ned and Blundertail to stay with him as he headed east, *away* from Halcyon.

"As the story begins, the travelers were walking down a road much like this one," Andrew said. "Pointynog held a torch high. Snicknik anxiously circled the group. Snicknik raced ahead, darted back, ran into the woods, got lost, and came back again."

"That is just like him," Blundertail said. "He could be so silly!"

"When he returned, the group had moved on," Andrew said. He was *so* happy to be telling a story that did not involve him—and to have such an appreciative audience! "Snicknik squinted in the gathering darkness and saw a dim, bumpy light in the distance. He thought it would be no challenge at all to catch up with his friends, so he ran toward them. But no matter how fast he ran, the light remained the same distance ahead."

"Could it be some form of magic?" Blundertail asked. "I believe there is such a thing in the world. How can you hear a child's first laugh and not believe it?"

"I think it was something else," Andrew said. "And so did Snicknik. He simply didn't know what. Hours later, he was nearing exhaustion. Finally, he saw that the distance between himself and the light was lessening. He drove himself onward, the muscles in his legs tingling with exertion. Then he began hearing odd sounds, like the creak and rumble of a carriage."

Andrew hesitated. For a moment he thought *he* had heard those sounds. Only they were *behind* him, not ahead as in the story.

"Snicknik felt foolish," Andrew said. "He *had* been chasing a carriage, one drawn by swift-footed saurians!"

"Of course," Blundertail said. "I should have seen it coming. Very good, very good indeed. So delightful."

Andrew continued. "As Snicknik approached the dim glow, he saw light multiplying quickly as lanterns were lit. The travelers were making camp. Meanwhile, his friends were almost certainly in the forest or on the road looking for him. Snicknik decided that sooner or later they would pick up his scent if he simply stayed in one place. And so he approached the travelers, who were pitching camp...."

Andrew's voice trailed off, and he turned to look back. He was certain of it now. He *did* hear the sounds of a carriage. And in the distance was a tiny amber glow—just like the one Snicknik had been following. Andrew scratched his head, wondering what was going on.

"Listen," Andrew said.

"We are listening," Blundertail replied. "When does the singer come into the tale?"

"He's at the camp," Andrew said absently. "Snicknik heard the singer's voice as he approached. The singer delivered a song of joy and thanks that created such wonder in Snicknik, such an array of emotions, that the usually speedy knight actually took his time reaching the camp. He didn't want the song to be brought to a halt because of his unexpected arrival."

"Good thinking," Blundertail said.

"Actually, it was amazing that Snicknik had stopped to think things through," Andrew said. "Not quite a first, but certainly something that didn't happen every day."

Andrew heard sounds exactly like those he had described in his story. A carriage was approaching!

As the carriage neared, Andrew saw that it was

drawn by two Ceratosaurus and was relatively small. The Ceratosaurus both had huge heads, short thick arms, and long muscular legs. They had sleek torsos and looked more trim than any Tyrannosaurus, which they vaguely resembled. Each sported a bony horn on his snout.

Two figures could be seen on the carriage's roof. One was human, and the other was a saurian who lay on a resting couch atop the carriage.

A lantern was raised, and Andrew saw Lian waving! She had decided to come with them after all!

Chirping sounds that might have been singing rose in the night air. Andrew recognized the noise as the chattering of the Ceratosaurus hauling the carriage. Soon he could make out words. The Ceratosaurus were challenging one another to go faster.

"Move, slow-foot!"

"Slow-foot? You're all but a tail-dragger! Try and catch me!"

Andrew waved his torch, but the carriage didn't slow. It wouldn't stop. They had to get out of the road!

"Goodness," Blundertail said. "This isn't safe." The old dinosaur whirled his tail, striking the back of Andrew's legs. Andrew fell and hit his head on a rock embedded in the road. He moaned and tried to rise, but he felt dazed. The earth thundered, and heavy trampling feet approached.

The carriage was coming right for him!

CHAPTER 8

Andrew's head ached, and he was only barely aware of what was going on. He felt strong hands grab him, pick him up by the tunic, and rush him to the side of the road. He heard the carriage race past, its wheels scraping and straining, the saurians who pulled it chattering madly while the human and the saurian above shouted to get their attention. Finally, he heard the carriage slow and stop some distance away.

Ned crouched beside him, checking his head for wounds. "You're not bleeding. I think you'll be all right."

"Those tremors are getting worse with every moment," Blundertail said. "I might think it was the Great Dragon pounding away in his underground stone keep, but you said he has been awakened. Is he trapped again? Did Snicknik trap him as Ripclaw once did?"

Andrew sighed. He reached up and felt a small bump on his forehead.

"I think the story will have to wait," Ned said. "Let's get to that carriage."

Ned helped Andrew to his feet, and Lian came running.

"Is he all right?" she asked, pointing at Andrew.

"Oh, I'm sure," Ned said. "He has a pretty hard head, after all. At least lately."

Andrew winced, more from Ned's words than from the pain he felt. But he knew he deserved it.

"I'm sorry," Andrew said.

Ned grinned. "Apology accepted."

Ned took one of Andrew's arms while Lian supported him on the other side. Together they helped Andrew to the carriage.

"I am so excited to learn more about Snicknik and the mysterious singer he meets on the road," Blundertail said. "But sometimes anticipation is a storyteller's greatest tool. Don't you think so, Andrew?"

"Ummm," Andrew said. He felt as if he might not make it to the carriage without falling into unconsciousness. But soon he was there.

Ned and Lian loaded Andrew into the carriage, resting him on one of the two cushioned couches within. There was a brief discussion, and Andrew heard something about Ned and Blundertail sitting on the rear bumper. Then he heard a command, and Lian climbed inside with him. She closed the door as the carriage rolled forward.

At first the jarring movement kept him awake, but

then Lian stroked his forehead and whispered, "Sleep."

He had never been able to say no to anything Lian told him.

Andrew woke to find the carriage still in motion. He was surprised. Had they ridden all night? Sunlight was streaming in through small windows in the carriage doors. Lian lay curled in the opposite resting couch. Andrew was starved. He yawned, stretched, and felt a flash of pain in his head. The discomfort ebbed quickly as he sat up. Lian awoke instantly.

"Are you all right?" Lian asked.

Andrew nodded. He still felt a slight ache in his head, but that was all. His stomach suddenly rumbled, and they both laughed.

"Well, you've got your appetite back," Lian said. "That's a good sign after all this time."

Andrew shook his head. He looked out the window. "It's only morning."

"Late afternoon, actually," she said. "I stayed up the entire night watching over you and only got to sleep a few hours ago." She moved her head from side to side. "I can tell how long I've been out from how stiff my neck is. These couches aren't the most comfortable I've ever used, but you know what they say: 'Never question good fortune.'"

Andrew understood. Lian had been raised as the

daughter of a great man in China. Growing up, she had known comfort and privilege. She had told Andrew often enough that she had loathed all the trappings of wealth. And he knew for a fact that she had longed to be a warrior like her brothers. Her adventures in the lost city of Halcyon had caused her to lay down her sword. Still, there were times when he suspected she wouldn't mind just a touch of the sophisticated lifestyle she once had known.

He wondered if she might enjoy a visit to one of the larger cities on the island, like Waterfall City or Sauropolis. He had been to both recently. But he sensed this was not the time to bring it up.

"So this carriage was just passing through town?" Andrew asked.

"The carriage master stopped at your father's place for a meal," Lian said. "He doesn't talk much. His name's Gralph. I *think*. That and Sparklebrook were the two words I could make out from his gruntings. I thought, well, *Sparklebrook,* that's along our way, so..."

"Never question good fortune."

"Right."

Lian turned and hammered on the thick wooden wall behind her. The carriage slowed and soon came to a stop. Lian got out first and offered her hand to Andrew. He was still a little wobbly, so he let her help him down.

The group gathered by the side of the road, and Andrew ate a meal of sweet bread and berries. Everyone carried freshwater in canteens.

Blundertail's armor creaked and moaned as he stretched. He nodded toward Andrew. "You'll be happy to know that there have been no more of those nasty earthquakes since you fell. I think that may have been the last of them!"

The carriage master looked up. He was a Herrerasaurus, a ten-foot-long bipedal dinosaur with a box-shaped head, a rounded snout, and a pair of bumpy ridges near his eyes. His kind was one of the earliest dinosaurs ever to walk the planet. He had orange scales with brownish stripes, and a beautiful silver medallion dangled from a chain on his wrist.

"Earthquakes?" the carriage master asked in a low growl. He was studying his medallion.

"Oh, yes," Blundertail said. "They've been quite strong the past day or so. And they leave such messes in their wake!"

Andrew caught Ned watching him. He shrugged and smiled. Ned relaxed.

Let Blundertail think there were earthquakes and not realize that he's the one making all these messes, Andrew thought. *What harm can it do?*

As if in answer to his question, Andrew felt his head throb again.

"Earthquakes," Gralph said again. He grunted and walked toward the saurians hauling the carriage.

Andrew studied the vehicle. Carriages like this one were a rare sight on Dinotopia. They were designed for speed and were used when a human or saurian who was afraid of flying had to reach a certain destination quickly. Andrew wondered who in Sparklebrook could be in need of such a conveyance. He hoped that nothing was wrong—and that he had not slowed them down too much.

"So," Blundertail said. "Andrew was in the midst of telling us a story!"

"Really?" Lian asked. "What kind of story?"

Her interest invigorated him. He quickly told her what had happened already in the story, then went on with the adventure of Snicknik and the great singer.

"Of all the absent members of the Explorers Club, Snicknik missed Pointynog the most," Andrew said. "Snicknik was often heard to remark, 'Pointynog, you are Brain. I am just Feet. I race everywhere without a care and sometimes get into trouble as a result. What could Feet be without Brain?'"

Lian and Ned laughed at this. Blundertail leaned on a rock and waited excitedly for Andrew to continue.

"You see, Snicknik had a very good sense of things that were going on around him," Andrew said. "His instincts were very sharp. He had a feeling that the situation he was walking into was one that would require Brain. And he was just Feet!"

"I think Snicknik had wisdom he didn't know he

possessed!" said Blundertail.

Andrew smiled and nodded. "As do most knights of the Unrivaled."

Blundertail raised his chin, looking very pleased.

"The sound of Snicknik's clanking armor announced his presence before he could say a word," Andrew said. "The humans at the camp looked up at his arrival. All but the singer and a young man with a mournful expression jumped to their feet out of respect for the visiting knight. The singer appeared too preoccupied to worry about protocol, and the young man to whom he sang seemed too lost in his own sadness to care."

"What made him sad?" Blundertail asked.

Andrew took a bite of sweet bread. He looked away, building dramatic effect—and buying himself enough time to finish his food.

"Why was the young man sad?" Lian asked.

Andrew smiled inwardly. He had hoped this turn in the story would capture her interest.

"Well, as much as Snicknik said he wasn't a thinker, he *did* think about that," Andrew said. "Everyone waited until the singer had finished his song, and then introductions were made. It turned out that they were a group of farmers. They were traveling to share the knowledge they had gained of working the land in the days before they came to Dinotopia."

"They were dolphinbacks!" Blundertail said. "An entire family of dolphinbacks."

Andrew nodded.

"And farmers," Lian said. Her expression became a little sad. "I wonder what it's like to plant a crop and see it grow."

Andrew knew that he had to tread carefully now. It was no accident that he had chosen to tell this particular version of this story.

"The young man's name was Terrance," Andrew said. "And he was sad because he wanted to be at harmony with the earth like the other members of his family. But he had a restless streak. He became distracted easily, and he found himself bored during the long hours he spent tilling fields and planting crops with his family."

"What about the singer?" Lian asked. "It seemed he had a calling that had nothing to do with the land."

"That was another reason why Terrance was sad," Andrew explained. "He thought that of all people, his older brother Gerard would understand. With his voice, Gerard could become a great bard. Maybe the greatest Dinotopia had ever known! But all Gerard dreamed of was working the fields and tending his crops. He sang to give thanks to nature and to voice the happiness that was in his heart when he was doing the work he loved."

"And this is the man whose singing wakes the dragon," Blundertail said. "The Great Dragon of the Outer Dark!"

"His singing does more than wake the dragon," Andrew said. "But that comes later in the story. What's important now is Terrance. He felt he had no direction. He knew what he *didn't* want to do with the rest of his life, but he had no idea what he *did* want to do. For a time, he had tried the way of the earth. He had given himself over to it completely. But it just wasn't for him."

"Yes," Lian said distractedly. "The key to happiness is having dreams. The key to success is making dreams come true. But what if you don't have a dream? If you don't know what you want?"

The carriage master returned. He nodded toward the sun. Andrew could see now that it was indeed afternoon.

"Leaving," the carriage master grunted. "Now."

"The rest of the story will have to wait," Andrew said.

"I'll be curious to hear how it turns out for Terrance," Lian said.

"It will turn out well," Blundertail said reassuringly. "All tales turn out well on Dinotopia!"

Andrew smiled. He believed in what Blundertail was saying. But judging from the look on Lian's face, he worried that she did not.

CHAPTER 9

They arrived at the small village of Sparklebrook just before sunset. The streets were crowded with busy humans and saurians. The carriage master leaped down from the conveyance and disappeared into the crowd without a word.

"How very odd," Blundertail said.

"He may be racing to pick up whomever he has to transport," Andrew offered. "When he gets back, we'll ask where he's heading next. Maybe he'll have room to take us."

"Why ask him?" one of the Ceratosaurus hauling the wagon said. "He wouldn't know. Next stop, Pooktook!"

Andrew stepped around to the front of the carriage and placed his hand on the shoulder of the dinosaur who had spoken.

"I don't understand," Andrew said. "If Gralph wasn't the carriage master, who is?"

The Ceratosaurus wobbled his head and rolled his eyes. "There are so many possibilities left."

"*You're* the carriage master?"

"He thinks he is," replied the other Ceratosaurus quickly. "But only because I know he needs his little daydreams."

"Then who was Gralph?"

"Our passenger!" the saurians replied in unison. "Do you wish to go to Pooktook?"

"No," Andrew said. "That's back the way we came and then some."

"Off with the lot of you, then," the Ceratosaurus said. The horn on his snout glinted in the sun. "We are busy, busy, busy!"

Andrew and the others stood back as the saurians turned the carriage. A flash of light from the resting couch above caught everyone's attention.

"Hold!" Blundertail cried. His voice boomed with as much knightly authority as he could muster, but the two carriage masters did not respond to his command.

Lian leaped forward, jumping onto the carriage's rear bumper. She stole over the top of the carriage with flawless grace, snatched something from the resting couch, and leaped off as the carriage gained speed. She flipped in midair and landed on her feet. Then the carriage sped off.

Lian held up the object she had snatched from the speeding carriage.

"It's Gralph's medallion!" Blundertail said.

"The clasp broke," Lian said. "He went off in such a hurry that I'm sure he doesn't know he left it behind."

"We have to get it back to him," Ned said. "It's the virtuous thing!"

"Yes, we must!" Blundertail agreed. "It is a task befitting a knight and his squire."

Ned snatched the medallion from Lian's hand. "See if you can find transportation east. We'll be back soon!"

Blundertail and Ned darted off and were quickly lost in the crowd.

Andrew looked around with Lian. Sparklebrook was a lovely village sandwiched between the shimmering Stillwater Creek and a series of hills not quite high enough to be called mountains—or even to be listed on most travelers' maps. But they were very pretty.

The streets were filled with groups of humans and saurians carrying large sacks and pushing heavy carts to and from an area at the base of the closest hill.

"I'm surprised no one's welcomed us," Andrew said. He was partially relieved. Their fellow traveler in the carriage and the two carriage masters had shown no interest at all in him or in hearing the tale of his adventure in Halcyon. Even better, for the first time in months, he'd been able to tell a made-up tale that held his audience spellbound. Yet he was still surprised and even a little disappointed by the way the villagers didn't seem to notice them.

"Everyone's so busy," Lian said.

Andrew laid his hand on the shoulder of a fast-moving Pachycephalosaurus.

"Chromedome's hurrying," the dinosaur said as he ground to a stop. His domelike head was streaked with rusty orange and dotted with emerald. The ridge around his skull was covered by flowers glued in place by dried sap. He wore a white frock and was weighed down by dozens of necklaces and chains.

"I can see you're hurrying. So is everyone else. Why? What's going on?" Andrew asked.

"The Annual Festival of Hooksnout," Chromedome said.

Lian looked surprised. "The great playwright?"

"He was born here," Chromedome said. "Today would have been his three hundred and tenth birthday!"

Andrew was surprised. His mentor had told him that Hooksnout had been born in Sparklebrook and that a festival was held for him every year. Andrew had been so wrapped up in his own problems that he hadn't bothered to find out when it was scheduled.

"We will enact *The Circle* in his memory," Chromedome said.

"That's one of his lesser-known plays," Andrew said. "But, from what I recall, it's a celebration of trust and harmony and—"

"Yes, yes," Chromedome said as he darted away.

"Trust is the most valuable thing you'll ever learn and so on and so forth. The day is a wonderful one! Much to do!"

Andrew put his hand up and called, "Thank you!"

The head-butting dinosaur sped off, darting through the crowded street.

"These people take their festival very seriously," Lian said. "Like it's the most important thing in their lives!"

Andrew nodded. He walked with Lian through the crowd and witnessed a surprising exchange.

"Costuming *is* more important," a Dilophosaurus said sweetly, as if she were making her point to a child. Her colorful dual crests wiggled in the wind, and she wore a cape that was painted with a kaleidoscopic, dizzying array of colors and patterns. "I think it is clear to all that I should have more assistants than you."

A meaty middle-aged woman in a black and green dress tapped the side of her face contemplatively. "Not to me. I'm in charge of the food, and I've seen from experience that if revelers aren't fed a hearty meal that sits well in their stomachs, they may not stay long enough to see all the pretty costumes. They'll all be on their feet, going to get more to eat long before the show is over. That's why I need more assistants than you!"

Andrew sensed that there was no true ill will between these two. They both sincerely wished to do their best to make this festival a success. But there was a true lack of harmony between them.

Andrew and Lian walked through the village, darting out of the way of the rushing humans and saurians. Everywhere they turned, the same scene was playing out: humans and saurians disagreeing over the smallest details of some performance scheduled for twilight. Finally, Andrew and Lian took a seat at a table outside a closed eatery.

"I don't think we'll get anyone to talk to us until the performance is over," Andrew said. "Maybe we should just stay and enjoy it with everyone else."

"I'll go with that," Lian said. "I just wish they were taking more pleasure in their preparations."

"'Remember the steam kettle,'" Andrew said, quoting from an old teacher they had shared.

"'Though up to its neck in hot water, it continues to sing!'" Andrew and Lian said in harmony. They laughed and laughed, and soon Lian's hand found Andrew's.

"So," she said, "are you going to tell me what happened with Terrance?"

"Not until the others are here," Andrew said. "It's a tale for all."

Lian frowned. "I suppose. I have to say I like your story, but I can't help noticing how certain parts of it seem to relate to each of us."

"I suppose it's just been a matter of coincidence and fortunate timing," Andrew said.

"You don't believe in fate any longer?" Lian asked. "And that everything happens for a reason?"

"I still believe in harmony," Andrew said. "And I guess I still believe that there's a reason for everything. But sometimes I get impatient waiting for the reasons to show themselves. Does that ever happen to you?"

"All the time."

They sat together quietly despite the fracas around them.

"What is the Outer Dark?" Lian asked suddenly. "I've never heard of such a place."

"It's not really a place," Andrew said. "It's more a state of mind. In the Outer Dark, we combat our greatest fears. Storytellers use the Outer Dark to symbolize an arena in which someone has to resolve an inner conflict."

"I don't know that I like the sound of that," Lian said.

"It's something we all have to face sooner or later," Andrew said. "But it can be overcome."

She nodded. "If you were a character in a story, what would be your Outer Dark?"

Andrew lowered his head. "Never being able to tell a story again. And you?"

Lian looked away. "I'll tell you after I hear more of your story."

Andrew saw that the sun was setting. The people of Sparklebrook were in more of a hurry than ever to reach the stage that had been set up at the base of the hill. They couldn't wait to see the play.

"Where are Ned and Blundertail?" Andrew asked, suddenly mindful of the time. "They shouldn't have had *that* much trouble finding Gralph."

Lian stood. "I'm sure they're all right. Maybe they've been drawn into helping the villagers with their play. Let's head over to the stage and see."

Andrew and Lian navigated through the rushing stream of villagers. They stopped beside a pair who were talking. Andrew hoped to overhear something that might give him a clue about his missing friends' whereabouts.

"Sparklebrook was Hooksnout's home," a young blond-haired man said. He was nearly out of breath. "Tonight's event must be perfect!"

He was speaking to a young, yellow-spotted duck-billed saurian. The dinosaur looked off distractedly. "I'm sorry, Philippe. Did you say something? I was thinking about the props. I hope they're all right. Every year it seems this festival becomes more difficult for all of us."

When he turned back, the young man was gone. The duck-billed saurian threw up his little hands in worry and ran off.

Andrew leaned in close to Lian. "Do you think maybe this performance might be important to the villagers?" he teased.

"Yes, but this is supposed to be a play about harmony, and those who are presenting it are not acting in any kind of harmony that I can see," Lian said. "I hope we find the Goblet of Gismore. I can see that it will have its uses!"

"I'm sure all will be well after the play is done," Andrew said. "People get distracted, and sometimes they focus on the wrong things. All will be well."

They searched the crowd for Ned and Blundertail. Finally, they had to start asking villagers. They didn't think it would be hard to find someone who had seen their companions. After all, how common could the sight of a Knight of the Unrivaled be?

But all the villagers were busy and distracted, and no one seemed to have noticed the pair.

Andrew sighed. He reached the stage and saw the pit for the musicians and the glaring lanterns set as footlights at the front of the stage.

The stage itself had been carved from the base of the hill, and a series of tunnels led off from the rocky "cavern" that had been created. Stalactites and huge boulders hung from above, held in place by thin lines controlled by humans and saurians, who were all but hidden from view on the flanks of the stage. Two sixty-foot-long Apatosaurus stood at opposite sides of the stage, wearing odd harnesses. The lines connected to their harnesses slid down into ditches that vanished into the ground.

"Excuse me," Lian said as she touched the arm of a

young girl handing out plates of warm pie. "Have you seen our friends? One is a Troodon in armor, an elderly warrior, holding a medallion—"

"The funny one!" the girl cried. "He went to the rear of the Sleeping Mountain."

Andrew looked up. "This hill."

"It's a *mountain!*" the girl cried.

"Yes," Lian said. "Our apologies. The Sleeping Mountain. Was he following someone?"

"Only Boomingvoice, one of the greatest saurian actors on the island!" the girl giggled. "He's playing Gralph, the saurian hermit who didn't bond with anyone until an earthquake trapped him in a cavern with a lonely dolphinback. Their efforts to free themselves slowly turn them into friends. Access to backstage is through the mountain."

Andrew and Lian stared at each other as the little girl gave them pie.

"Boomingvoice had to rush here to take the part of Gralph because his brother was sick." The girl looked around. "Pie, anyone?"

Andrew let her go and turned to Lian. "An earthquake."

"An actor," Lian added.

Music sounded, and they turned to the stage. A lone human in ragged clothing took the stage. Applause and great cheers erupted from the crowd.

"I am lost," the man said. "This place is strange

and frightening. Will I never see home again?"

Then, to Andrew's amazement, the man began to sing—*just* like in his story.

"There's going to be an earthquake," Andrew said, nodding toward the huge harness-wearing sauropods.

"And Blundertail is backstage."

Without another word, they broke from the crowd and ran to find the path leading to the rear of the Sleeping Mountain.

CHAPTER 10

Blundertail was overjoyed to be on his first knightly errand. Together with his squire, he had followed Gralph around the back of the Sleeping Mountain and through a narrow tunnel. Blundertail's great saurian sense of smell had allowed him to pick out Gralph's distinctive scent and trail it effortlessly.

Still, no matter how many times they had called out to Gralph, they had received no reply. And as fast as they ran after the saurian, they could not catch up to him. It reminded Blundertail of Andrew's story of Snicknik on the trail. Soon he was even hearing singing.

The tunnels were lit by a dull phosphorescence that clung to the ceiling. In the dim green glow, Blundertail turned to Ned. "Be careful. There are twists and turns ahead. I can tell from the way the air flows through these passages."

Ned nodded and slowed a little. Blundertail also slowed. Blundertail understood that it was important to return Gralph's medallion, but he did not want to make Ned feel inferior just because Ned lacked the natural speed and grace of a Knight of the Unrivaled!

"I wonder if this is what the tunnels leading to the lair of the Great Dragon of the Outer Dark are like," Blundertail said.

"I don't know," Ned said. "Wouldn't there be signs and symbols of warning all over the walls?"

"Yes, it would be so," Blundertail said thoughtfully. "You're a clever lad. You might make a great librarian one day!"

"I'm an inventor," Ned said. "And you're a Knight of the Unrivaled! The road that leads to dusty scrolls lies behind us."

"Agreed," Blundertail said wistfully. A plate from the left flank of his armor dropped off. He bent to pick it up, turning sharply, and heard Ned grunt and fall.

"Are you all right?" Blundertail asked.

"Oh, you know," Ned said. He stood and dusted himself off. "Earthquakes."

"Goodness, I wonder what causes them," Blundertail said.

"I think it could be some of the old machines of Dinotopia rumbling to life," Ned said.

"What a vivid imagination you have," Blundertail said. "But if you wish to be an inventor, then an inventor you should be."

"Idlecrest says the world is before us, and we need

not leave it as we found it," Ned said.

"Wise words," Blundertail said. "I have made my mark by teaching knights about the First Code of Chivalry. I've learned that it's important to keep alive the ancient traditions and historical documents, not only in dusty scrolls, but also in the hearts and minds of others. Perhaps now I will be the figure in just such a scroll. *If* your friend Andrew decides to write down our exploits."

"I'm sure he will," Ned said. "They will be too exciting for him to resist!"

"Onward, my squire!"

"Onward!" Ned echoed.

They raced ahead, the mournful singing growing louder.

"Such a sad song," Blundertail said. "And it is sung in a language I have never learned."

"It's an ancient human language," Ned said. "It sounds familiar from my lessons, but I can't quite place it."

They followed the twisting tunnel, Blundertail pausing at forks to sniff the air to find Gralph's scent.

Gralph. Hmmm. There was *something* familiar about that name. But what?

Blundertail turned a corner and was startled by the sight of a cavern filled with blinding light. The human who had been singing stood just ahead, looking out at the wall of light. He was swarthy and dressed in rags.

His beard was long and he looked as if he hadn't slept in days!

The human stopped singing and hung his head. "Alone. I am ever alone."

"No, *I'm* here!" Blundertail called as he stepped into the cavern, his heart going out to the forlorn man. "And so is my squire!"

Suddenly, shouts and strange cries arose. Blundertail wondered where all those voices were coming from. On top of that, there was such a strange mix of scents coming from the lighted area—scents identical to those he had detected in the village.

The man stared at Blundertail with wide eyes as another figure appeared at the far end of the cavern. It was Gralph! Only—he was making a shooing motion.

How *very* odd.

Blundertail clanked and banged as he strode onto the cavern floor. It felt strange to him. Uneven and unsettled. Not like a typical stone floor at all!

"Gralph!" Blundertail called. "We found your medallion. You left it in the carriage!"

Gralph's little arms went up and he motioned again for Blundertail to step back. Blundertail glanced about and saw no cause for the saurian's alarm.

"Ned, do you have any idea why they are acting so strangely?" Blundertail asked his squire.

"No," Ned said. "Except, wait! *Gralph.* Wasn't that the name of—"

"Rockfall!" a woman shouted from a darkened wing of the cavern.

Rockfall? Blundertail thought. There was no—

Suddenly, the ground began to tremble, and stones fell from above. Blundertail wobbled and nearly stumbled. He felt as if he stood on a carpet that was being shaken like a sheet after washing!

"The earthquake!" Blundertail shouted.

"I think it really is an earthquake this time!" Ned hollered back.

Blundertail didn't know what Ned meant. *This* time? They had been suffering the effects of earthquakes for days!

The ground shuddered, and rocks fell with thunderous crashes. This earthquake was the most powerful one yet!

Blundertail looked at the shuddering man before him. It was all so odd. Blundertail sensed that the man wasn't *really* frightened, yet he acted as if he were. And the danger about him was all too real!

"I will be buried in this alien land!" the man called.

Blundertail tilted down the visor on his helm. He would not let the man be harmed. He surged forward, noticing Gralph moving quickly from the other side of the cavern.

"No!" Gralph hollered. "Stop! I'll save him!"

Blundertail raced ahead and struck with his gauntleted hands at a large stone that was falling toward the bedraggled man. The boulder burst as if it were not a true rock at all, but mere clay. And *feathers* flew from within it. How very odd!

Blundertail clearly did not know his own strength. Even more wondrously, he had been granted some strange magic to turn dangerous objects into simple props, like those one might find on a stage.

He turned swiftly, heard a small cry, and looked down to see the bedraggled man crouching low, trying to protect his head. Blundertail struck at the falling stones, determined to do his duty well as a true Knight of the Unrivaled!

CHAPTER 11

Andrew and Lian arrived backstage just in time to see the disaster unfold in all its epic glory. Blundertail was on stage, sending fake rocks to their doom and nearly whacking the poor human actor on the head with his flying tail!

Boomingvoice stood nearby, his shoulders slumped. He allowed the props to fall on his head. The actor had abandoned the character of Gralph.

The footlights were being smashed by the remains of the falling "boulders," and Andrew could see the crowd's stunned expression just beyond the now-abandoned orchestra pit.

"Help!" the human actor shouted. "Someone help me!"

"Don't be afraid," Blundertail said. "I *am* helping you!"

Andrew heard cries and disappointed moans from the crowd. He squeezed Lian's hand and said, "We have to get Blundertail and Ned out of here."

Lian nodded. Ned was crouched nearby, digging through his bag. Andrew went to Blundertail, and Lian headed toward Ned.

"Blundertail!" Andrew called. He raised his hand to protect himself from the thin shards of clay that flew through the air as the Troodon knight battered the fake boulders.

The dinosaur looked up. "Andrew, this place isn't safe!"

Andrew felt the ground starting to level out. He understood now that the huge harness-wearing sauropods were pulling on wires and using their strength to make this false floor shudder and shake. Someone had finally given them—and the prop masters who were releasing the false stones—the cue to halt their efforts.

"It's safe now," Andrew said. "But there may be people hurt on the other side of the mountain." Andrew looked at Boomingvoice. "Don't you think so, Gralph?"

The actor sighed. "I suppose. Come!"

Blundertail hesitated. He didn't seem to notice the murmur of disappointment from the crowd. Instead, he looked down at the human actor.

"Tell everyone that a Knight of the Unrivaled saved you," the saurian said. "Tell them Blundertail the Bold was here!"

"I don't think they'll soon forget," the man said.

Andrew pulled on the saurian's arm. Blundertail

stopped and turned back. "Oh, and you have a very nice singing voice. If you wish to become a great singer, I believe you could. Idlecrest said that one's chances of success in any undertaking can always be measured by one's belief in oneself."

"Oh," the actor said with a little smile. "Thank you."

Andrew saw that Lian had Ned on his feet. Boomingvoice wandered in shock toward the tunnel leading out of the mountain.

"Look!" Andrew said to Blundertail. "Gralph's leaving. And you still need to return his medallion."

"Goodness, you're right," Blundertail said. "And there may be others who need my help!"

"Yes, indeed," Andrew said as he led Blundertail away. The small group navigated the tunnels and soon stood together at the rear of the mountain.

Blundertail scanned the horizon. "I don't think anyone was hurt. In fact, I don't see anyone at all. What a relief!"

Turning, Blundertail bowed and formally presented the actor with his lost trinket. "I have seen others look at objects like this with such intensity and fondness. I hope its restoration brings you joy."

Andrew was close enough now to see the medallion clearly. It bore an image of the scene Boomingvoice had been about to play out, a saurian saving a human from a rockfall.

It was a *prop*, Andrew realized. Something to help

the actor prepare for his performance.

Or was it something more? Boomingvoice stared at the medallion with genuine emotion.

"My brother gave me this, and now he is ill," Boomingvoice said. "I should go to him."

The actor walked away, avoiding the tunnel that led back to the stage.

"He didn't say thank you," Ned said.

"No thanks are needed," Blundertail said. "The reward for a good deed is to have done it."

Soon the saurian was taken by the darkness on this side of the great hill.

"Ah," Blundertail said. "We have performed well tonight. Perhaps we should see if there's an inn that has room for us."

Andrew exchanged glances with Ned, who shook his head and looked away. Andrew knew that Blundertail hadn't *meant* to ruin the performance the people of Sparklebrook had worked so hard to put on. He didn't even know he had done it!

"I think we should continue on," Andrew said. "The goblet is waiting, after all!"

"Too true," Blundertail said. "Besides, the past, present, and future are really one, according to Idlecrest. They are today. And so we shall go onward today."

Andrew and Lian led Blundertail and Ned in a wide arc around the village and back to the road, which led northeast to Camaraton and Wimple

Springs. They walked a half-dozen miles, then stopped at Stillwater Creek and fished for their dinner. Afterward, they ate and made camp.

"Ah, Andrew," Blundertail said, "I think it is time to hear more of your tale of Snicknik and the farmers. I so want to hear how Terrance's brother woke the Great Dragon of the Outer Dark! What happened when he did?"

Andrew looked at Ned. "Is this a time for story-telling?"

"A gentle story," Ned said. "Only that."

"Gentle?" asked Blundertail. "This is a story of robust adventure!"

"So it is," Andrew said. "But there is always quiet before the storm."

"There is a storm in this story?" Blundertail asked.

"Of a kind," Andrew said. "The group had stopped at Windy Point, above the Crystal Caverns."

Blundertail clicked his claws excitedly. "I've always wanted to visit the Crystal Caverns. And Windy Point, too!"

"It turns out," Andrew said, "that the secret tomb of the Great Dragon of the Outer Dark was just below where the travelers had made their camp."

"That's how the dragon hears the singer!" Blundertail exclaimed.

"Just so," Andrew agreed. "But it was never the singer's wish to wake the dragon. And there were signs of warning all around him. But he was so caught up in his own quest to bring cheer to his brother that he didn't realize what was happening about him."

"What kind of signs?" Blundertail asked.

"Well, when they were all very still, they could hear the wind, and it seemed to carry voices," Andrew said. "Like when we were in the cavern in Sparklebrook, I thought I heard voices from the brightly lit area. Didn't you?"

Blundertail nodded. "I heard something. And I smelled the scents of humans and saurians. There must have been a very odd wind blowing and some great drafts in that cavern!"

Andrew sighed. "I suppose." He bit his lip. He was trying to find a gentle way of making Blundertail understand what had actually happened back in Sparklebrook.

"What other signs were there?" Blundertail asked.

"Near the camp, there was a light," Andrew continued. "A great bright light. It was a reflection of their campfire on a stone that had been polished like glass by an intense flame. Like the kind a dragon of the Outer Dark might make."

"Ah," Blundertail said. "And like the great wall of light we faced this evening. What could that have been? I saw no flames that might have been reflected. Were there sunstones in the cavern?"

"I don't think so," Andrew said. "And there was one final sign. When the group went for an evening walk, Gerard tripped and fell against what looked like a heavy stone. But it cracked under his weight, as if it were made of soft clay."

"The same magic I witnessed this evening!" Blundertail said. "The very same. Hmmm. I wonder if there was something I should have noticed."

The dinosaur scratched his heavy brow against a nearby rock.

"No," Blundertail said. "Nothing comes to mind."

Andrew looked over at Ned. His brother leaned close and whispered, "Enough. We'll be careful. I promise. If anything else happens, I'll tell him myself. We'll just make sure nothing else happens."

Andrew clasped his brother's arm. What could he say? Ned's devotion to Blundertail was an inspiration.

A slow creaking of wooden wheels captured everyone's attention. They hurried back to the road and saw an enormous dung wagon approaching. Blundertail and Ned stood in its path, waving their arms.

The huge wagon, hauled by a seventy-foot-long sauropod, had a strong and distinctive odor. It was a Copro Cart, hauling a heavy load of dinosaur dung to the farmlands in the east.

A pair of richly dressed Copro Carters exited the wagon and came to greet the quartet. One was a large man with a red beard that reached down to his sternum and not a bit of hair on top of his head. His blue and white costume had a golden star at its heart. His companion was a Syntarsus. His body was narrow, with long legs like a stork. He also had three-fingered hands, a long bony tail, and sharp, curved teeth. He wore a robe embroidered with the same symbol as his companion's costume.

"We are in need of transportation," Blundertail said. "I am a Knight of the Unrivaled. This is my squire, Ned, and his friends Andrew and Lian."

"All are welcome," the Syntarsus said. "So long as you don't mind the subtle fragrance."

Andrew had ridden in Copro Carts before. He could handle the unique aroma. He tensed as he saw the bald man staring at him intently.

Oh, no, he thought. *If I'm recognized, I'll have to tell that other tale again!*

"I am Storklebeak," the Syntarsus said. "As for how I got the name, I'd say don't ask, it's a long story, but I love long stories and don't mind telling them!"

"Andrew is apprenticed to a master storyteller," Blundertail said. "He is in the midst of telling us a wondrous tale of the Explorers Club and how a singer woke the Great Dragon of the Outer Dark."

"Mmmm," the red-bearded man said. He smiled appreciatively.

"This is my friend Jonathan," Storklebeak said. "He doesn't speak. He can't. Or won't. He does seem content to listen, though!"

The red-bearded man nodded jovially.

"So," Storklebeak said, "do you wish to ride east with us?"

Blundertail looked toward the hills in the distance.

"Naturally, we will go forward. As Idlecrest said in his *Book of Wisdom,* 'No one gets to live life backward. Look ahead. That's where your future lies.'"

"'And hope is one of the principal springs that keeps us in motion,'" Ned added with a hearty laugh. "For me, hope and the future are one and the same."

Andrew nodded. Lian took his hand and walked with him as they all climbed on board.

CHAPTER 12

Andrew was excited about the prospect of having two new audience members for his tale of Snicknik and the dragon. He sat in the well-ventilated living room of the huge wagon with Lian, Blundertail, Ned, and the Copro Carters.

The only problem was that he couldn't get a word in! Storklebeak was as good as his promise. Better. The story of how he got his name was evidently a good bedtime story, because Jonathan was nodding off already, and Ned looked close behind!

"And there I was, floating in the water with only my snout piercing the waterline as everyone searched and searched for me," Storklebeak said. "Clever, I was. And crafty, too!"

Andrew felt his own eyelids growing heavy. Lian kicked his boot. He sat up straight and smiled.

"What happened next?" Andrew asked.

"Next is the tale of the one who found me and

gave me my name," Storklebeak said. "You see, he was born decades earlier…."

Andrew's smile faded. Storklebeak had already recounted four other family histories to better "set the tone" and "add flavor" to his tale.

Andrew was never going to get a chance to tell his story!

He listened, doing his best to concentrate on Storklebeak's words, but again he felt himself drifting off. He heard a little snore beside him, a soft, lilting sound. It was Lian.

Leaning against her shoulder, he said, "Oh, really?" and, "I wouldn't have guessed," and, "You don't say!" here and there as Storklebeak's tale wound on and on.

Suddenly, shafts of bright light shone in his face. He shook himself awake and saw that it was morning. The wagon had stopped, and the snore of the long-neck who had been hauling it sounded like a great horn in the distance.

Storklebeak was still on his feet, gesturing excitedly with his claws. "And that, my good, kind friends, is the tale of how I got my name!"

Andrew nudged Lian with his arm. She rocketed awake and followed suit as he applauded. Jonathan, Ned, and Blundertail also woke and clapped.

They left the wagon and set up a little camp for breakfast. Hills and valleys stretched across the horizon. The hilltops were streaked with pink and gold. A slight breeze blew. It looked as if it was going to be a beautiful day.

Andrew squinted. "I don't see the road."

"Oh, we often make our own route," Storklebeak said. "The road's around here somewhere. I'm sure Braveback, our carrier, can find it without any difficulty."

Andrew grinned with relief. He brushed down his messy hair, wishing for a place to bathe. Then he ate his morning feast with the others.

"I suppose everyone would like to hear what happens next with the great singer who woke the Great Dragon of the Outer Dark," Andrew said.

"Yes, do tell!" Blundertail said. Beside him, Lian nodded, her eyes shining with excitement. Ned was yawning, still waking up, but he gestured for Andrew to go on.

Storklebeak and Jonathan were peering at Braveback, the longneck.

"There is a story about that one," Storklebeak said. "A story filled with wonder and adventure. I don't know that it's a true story, but I know that I never get tired of hearing it. Or telling it, as the case may be."

Andrew's shoulders drooped. "You don't want to hear my story?"

"Braveback the Mighty, he is called," Storklebeak said. "But not always. Not when he was a baby. Back then he was called Itchyscritch. Do you know why?"

Sighing, Andrew said, "No."

"But you wish to," Storklebeak said. "I can tell. Who wants to hear about dragons and knights when you can hear a tale about someone right in your midst?"

Andrew was frustrated, but the words of his mentor came to him: *Nothing is as strong as gentleness or as gentle as strength.*

"Please, tell your story," Andrew said.

After all, he thought, *how long can a tale about a longneck take?*

"It all began *centuries* ago," Storklebeak said. "With a single egg that, unlike the proverb, did roll far from its nest. And in this egg was Braveback's great-grandfather, who hatched lost and alone, never knowing his kin…"

"What a sad beginning," Blundertail said. "Did he ever find his family?"

"That would be telling," Storklebeak said. "Which I will. In *time.*"

As the tale went on, Andrew saw that Lian and Ned became enraptured. And Jonathan, who must have heard the story dozens of times before, sat at full attention.

Storklebeak kept talking as they woke Braveback and fed him from the supply of greens they kept in a special section of the wagon. Andrew only half-listened, anxious to have his turn at storytelling. Soon they were back in the wagon, and Andrew was no longer listening to Storklebeak at all.

Lian leaned over and whispered, "You're pouting."

"No, I'm not," Andrew said crossly.

She tickled him, and he batted her hands away. "You're one big pout. A giant pout with a cute little snout."

He tried to pull back but couldn't as she kissed his nose. He tried to force the smile back, but it stole across his face.

"Hah! See?" she asked. "I made you smile. I knew I could."

"Take time to laugh," Blundertail said. "It is the music of the soul!"

Ned patted him on the arm. "Time is a river without banks. We must honor our hosts. Besides, it *is* a good story."

Andrew knew that Ned was referring to Storklebeak's tale, not his.

"And onward they marched, the great herd of duckbills, with the one who thought he was a part of the tribe and couldn't understand why his neck was so much longer than theirs," Storklebeak said. "How could they know that just ahead terrible danger waited?"

Andrew started drumming his fingers. He'd had time to work out exactly what would happen next in his story, and he wanted to tell it!

"The predators surrounded the herd, which took refuge in a deep lagoon," Storklebeak said. "But Braveback's ancestor could not follow them into the water. What was he to do?"

"He faces down the predators and uses his tail as a whip for the first time," Andrew said. "They run off, and he discovers the truth about himself—that he is different but has a unique value, just as all of us do."

Silence filled the little room, broken only by the groans and creaks of the wagon. Storklebeak regained his composure first.

"Yes, that's right!" Storklebeak said. "You're very clever."

"He *is* apprenticed to a master storyteller," Blundertail said. "Did I mention that?"

Storklebeak laughed. "Well, in any case, this is just the beginning of the tale. There is still Braveback's grandfather, father, and Braveback himself to chronicle. But I will get to that in good time. Be of good cheer."

Andrew was not of good cheer. He wanted to tell a story. And he'd been doing just that—until Storklebeak stole his audience!

"I bet you wouldn't be so interested in telling the tale of Braveback if you knew the stories I have to tell," Andrew said.

"Of course I would," Storklebeak said cheerily. "There is a time for all things and for all stories. As a storyteller, you must know that."

More of Talltail's words came to Andrew: *It is the tale, not he who tells it, that is important.*

Andrew rose. "I am Andrew Lawton, and it is because of me that the Knights of the Unrivaled have stepped into the light and once again protect Dinotopia. That is my story. Can you honestly tell me you'd rather continue telling this dry old history, which may or may not be history, than hear of my adventure from my own lips?"

From the corner of his eye, Andrew saw redbearded Jonathan look away sadly and shake his head. He saw Ned and Lian staring at him in shock.

But why? All he had done was try to spare them more of Storklebeak's ramblings.

"Oh," Storklebeak said. "You are *that* Andrew Lawton."

Within minutes, the wagon had stopped, and the quartet of adventurers stood outside as Jonathan and Storklebeak waved to them from the departing vehicle.

"Clearly, we are not worthy to travel in such lofty company as Andrew Lawton, liberator of the Unrivaled," Storklebeak said. "Best that we go before we can do you a further disservice."

Then the wagon rolled off, leaving its former passengers to search for something that even vaguely resembled a road.

"I think this is for the best," Andrew said. "Who knows how far we've been taken out of our way!"

No one spoke to him.

"I mean, if Braveback went in the kind of circles Storklebeak did, we could be right back where we started."

The soft howl of the wind was the only sound. That and the creaking of Blundertail's armor as the knight fidgeted a little.

"There is no duty so underrated as the duty of being happy," Blundertail said.

"Right," Andrew said. "So we'll make the best of it. All we have to do is find the road, and we'll be fine."

Lian took Ned's arm and nodded toward a series of hills to her left. "We'll search that way. Clearly, you don't need us for anything else. It's not as if we were there when you liberated Halcyon or anything."

Andrew shook his head. "What are you talking about?"

"You said your problem is that other people only want to hear you talk about your adventure in the lost city," Ned said.

"You heard all that?" Andrew asked. "You were awake?"

"I don't think the problem is with your audiences," Ned said. "I think the problem is with you."

Ned stormed off, and Lian fell in beside him.

"I just wanted to tell a story," Andrew said. "That's what I do. It's who I am!"

His friends never slowed as they climbed a nearby rise and vanished over its crest.

CHAPTER 13

Andrew felt very sorry for the way he had acted. Blundertail set one gauntleted claw on his shoulder.

"Ned will calm down," Blundertail said. "He spent a lot of time standing before the forges of Silverclaw. That kind of heat builds up in a body. All will be well. Besides, I've taught him well in the seven knightly virtues."

Andrew walked with Blundertail to the crest of a nearby hill. A small pond lay at the base of the hill, and leaves from a fallen tree floated on its surface.

"I know about honor and glory," Andrew said.

They reached the pond, and Blundertail crouched beside it. With one claw, he fished out a strong, wet leaf. "Ah, but that is only one of the seven. There is also valor to consider. And devotion and loyalty. Then benevolence, courtesy and respect, rectitude, and most important, complete honesty."

Andrew repeated that last one. "Complete honesty."

Blundertail pulled a tiny metal needle from his armor and rubbed it on his gauntlet. Then he set it on the leaf. Andrew watched as the needle turned first one way and then another, finally settling on a single direction and maintaining it no matter how Blundertail turned.

"The needle is magnetized," Blundertail said. "It will point north. This shall help us find the road."

Andrew noticed something at the crest of another hill. "That might help, too."

He pointed at a large rail sticking out of the ground with a signpost attached at the top. They walked toward it.

"So—do you think Ned is right?" Andrew asked. "I know I should have been more patient with Storklebeak. I just so wanted to tell my story."

"And I would dearly love to hear it," Blundertail said. "But I think Ned and Lian will be disappointed if we don't wait for them."

Andrew nodded. He couldn't believe what he had done. He had so wanted to tell a tale—any tale—that he had attempted to use the tale he least wished to tell just to get attention. And look where it had gotten him!

Oh. You are that *Andrew Lawton.*

He wondered what Storklebeak had meant by that. And he wondered about one other thing…

"How did Storklebeak get his name?" Andrew

asked. "I know what a stork is, but not a storkle. And he has a snout, not a beak!"

"Ah, you must have dozed," Blundertail said. "You see, his uncle found him when he was playing *catch me if you can,* but the saurian had a bad toothache. Everything he said sounded funny. He tried to name the young saurian Snorkelsnout, because he was using his snout as a snorkel, but the word just wouldn't come out right. The best anyone could make of it was Storklebeak, and since he was the one who found the child, it stuck!"

Andrew laughed. It was a good story. He wished he had applied the seven virtues when listening to his host's tale. He even wondered how things finally turned out for Braveback in his tale. Now he would never know.

They reached the top of the second hill and studied the signpost. The symbol painted on the sign was in a language neither of them could decipher, but the arrow beside it clearly stated its purpose.

Blundertail turned suddenly, his tail whacking the signpost. The sign spun and changed direction. Andrew was about to say something, but he considered the seven knightly virtues and kept silent. He tried to remember exactly which way the sign had pointed originally, but he couldn't.

Another sign beckoned in the distance. He decided that he would find some way to investigate that one without letting Blundertail too close to it.

"I think these signs are the key to reaching the road," Andrew said.

"The road bears to the east," Blundertail said as he held out the compass he had made. "If we walk in that direction, we should come across it easily."

Andrew was only half-listening to the elderly dinosaur. He saw a mystery in these signs and symbols, one that intrigued him greatly. He thought of the warnings he had described in his tale about the dragon's lair.

Andrew walked in a very wide arc around the second sign. If only he could understand the strange symbols. He stepped away, trying to understand why anyone would use such an uncommon language. Then he heard a whack and turned to see the signpost spinning. Andrew fixed the sign to the way he thought it had been pointing, but again he wasn't sure.

They kept walking, traveling a mile this time, until Blundertail stumbled midway down another hill and struck a third signpost as he struggled to keep his grip on his compass.

"We *are* heading east," Blundertail said, raising the leaf.

Andrew didn't bother to adjust this sign. He had no idea which way it was supposed to face. He decided that once he reached the closest town, he would find someone to tell so the signs could be fixed. At least he would solve their mystery!

"Sometimes I feel like Snicknik," Blundertail said with a sigh. "Not that I am a great knight. I know that I have much to do to earn that title. My good deed in Sparklebrook is just the beginning."

"Yes," Andrew said, thinking hard about that.

"But I do sympathize with the way Snicknik considers himself just Feet. In Halcyon, I am known for doing what others tell me, not for coming up with ingenious plans like those Ned so often devises. I often feel that everyone but me has Brain. Especially Ned."

Blundertail spoke with a pride and devotion toward his squire that was altogether worthy of a knight. But it saddened Andrew to hear Blundertail speak of himself in such a way.

"You said you believed Snicknik possessed wisdom he didn't realize he had," Andrew said. "I think the same can be said for you, Sir Blundertail."

The aged knight stopped. "You are the first to address me that way!"

"Then it's the first thing I've done right today, and for that much, anyway, I'm glad," Andrew said.

They headed east. Andrew was unable to contain his curiosity about the markers they encountered. He knew he should restrain himself with Blundertail following him so closely, but he found that he could not. The signs spun crazily, but this closer examination gave Andrew no further clues to their meaning.

"I think they look like feet," Blundertail said.

Andrew frowned. "Feet?"

"Yes," the knight said. "The symbols look like little feet!"

When they came to the next marker, Andrew examined it closely and saw that Blundertail was right! The symbols were exactly like saurian footprints. They were so varied that Andrew had not made the connection.

It was strangely similar to what he had concocted in his story.

"We are what and where we are because we first imagined it," Blundertail said.

Andrew turned to him. "Yes. I think you're right."

Before Andrew could say anything else, thunder sounded in the distance. Andrew looked at the sky. It was a clear, sunny day. Blue skies and no clouds.

"You don't think it's another earthquake, do you?" Blundertail asked.

Andrew didn't know what to say. He could feel vibrations beneath his feet. He looked at the land, picturing it splitting open before them.

"We have to make sure Ned and Lian are safe!" Andrew said.

Blundertail raised his compass. "We've traveled east all this time. If we head west, we should find them!"

The duo raced to the top of a crest, the ground shuddering beneath them. As they ran through valleys and over hills, the earth shuddered and quaked even more violently than before!

They were at the base of a valley midway back to their starting point when the growls and howls of stampeding dinosaurs reached their ears.

Blundertail froze and looked at his compass. "I hear them coming from the north. The south. And the west!"

Andrew heard them, too. He looked up as the first group of stampeding dinosaurs crested the ridge just behind them. Two other groups appeared from other directions. The saurians rushed down the hill, heading right for the spot where Blundertail and Andrew stood!

CHAPTER 14

The dinosaurs pouring into the valley on almost all sides did not look frightened. In fact, they seemed to be having a wonderful time!

"Red team wins," howled a speeding Tenontosaurus from the north. Crimson ribbons fluttered in the wind as he ran, hooked to jewelry he wore along his back.

"Blue team takes the prize," yelled a duck-billed Edmontosaurus from the south, his streamers a lovely shade of blue.

"No one's quicker than green," hollered an Iguanodon from the west as he roared with laughter. Beautiful emerald streamers flowed from the trinkets adorning his scales.

"The signs," Andrew whispered. "It's a footrace!"

"Why are they all converging?" Blundertail asked. The old saurian didn't realize that he had spun so many signs around, aiming all the teams in opposing directions.

"It doesn't matter why," Andrew said. "We have to get out of the way!"

Blundertail lowered his creaky visor. "Get to safety, young Andrew. I must do what I can to avert disaster. It is a knight's calling."

Andrew took a few steps back. What was Blundertail thinking?

"Gentle friends! Look up! Be aware!" Blundertail called. "You may harm yourselves or others!"

But all the competitors had their heads down and were shouting so loudly they heard only themselves. Even worse, they weren't looking where they were going. None of them realized what was about to happen.

"Blundertail, they can't hear you!" Andrew called.

"Perhaps not," said the knight. "But there must be another way." Blundertail looked down and saw bright sunlight glinting off a single shiny piece of his armor.

"Quickly, Andrew," Blundertail said. "Help me, then please get to safety." Blundertail fumbled with a series of clasps that held his breastplate in place.

Andrew felt the ground buckling beneath him, just as it had onstage at Sparklebrook. But what they had experienced there had been a performance, and *this* was real. He wasn't quite sure what Blundertail was up to, but he helped the elderly Troodon remove his breastplate.

"Now run!" Blundertail cried.

Each of the teams was less than a thousand yards away. Considering their great speed, it would be only a matter of moments before they collided.

Blundertail grasped the breastplate and tilted it so that sunlight struck the armor directly. He aimed the light into the eyes of the dinosaurs approaching from the north.

The dinosaur in the lead cried out in surprise. He looked up and shouted, "Stop, everyone! Stop!"

Blundertail angled the light toward the west, then toward the south.

Cries of "Halt!" sounded from all three directions. Dinosaurs stumbled as earth and rock were kicked up by the feet of behemoths. Clouds of dust rose from every direction. Andrew was frozen with fear. Blundertail threw him down and leaped over him. Then the collision came.

Andrew heard crashes, roars, growls, explosions. He felt as if a landslide had descended and buried both of them. The earth trembled in protest.

Finally, it was over. He heard moans and groans.

"Get off! Get off!" saurians wailed.

Andrew felt the crushing weight of Blundertail's armor biting into his back.

"I think if you crawl straight ahead, you can get clear of this," Blundertail whispered to him.

The saurian pushed himself upward, releasing the pressure on Andrew's back. Andrew did as the knight instructed, crawling for twenty feet before he escaped the smelly, scaly mass of wobbling, dazed saurians.

When he stood, he saw Lian and Ned racing down the hill toward them.

"Are you all right?" Lian asked.

"Blundertail!" Ned cried.

They waited as the huge pile of saurians sorted itself out. Only a few dinosaurs had bumps and bruises. There were no broken bones, no real injuries. Finally, Blundertail was uncovered.

The elderly knight's armor had some dents that it had not possessed before, and he seemed a bit dazed, but he was otherwise unharmed.

"You, gentle knight, must never consider yourself just Feet *ever again,*" Andrew said.

"Do you think our adventures would make a fine tale one day, Andrew?" Blundertail asked timidly.

"A very fine tale," Andrew said. "But I don't think I deserve the honor of telling it."

"How did this happen?" Ned asked.

"Our path was clear," said one of the dinosaurs with a green banner.

"So was ours. It was properly marked," cried one from the blue team. "We just followed the signs."

Blundertail looked perplexed. "Something must have turned them. There is a strong wind."

"Yes, it must have been the wind," said the leader of the blue team. "It does seem very strong."

"Agreed," said one of the Tenontosaurus representing the green team.

"The vibrations we made by running so quickly could have turned the signs," another dinosaur added. "Look, some of the signs are still spinning!"

Ned looked at Andrew imploringly. His brother wanted to know who was responsible. Andrew knew it was his fault. Blundertail might have turned the signs, but only because Andrew kept leading him to them!

Andrew turned his face away in shame.

"Ah," Ned said. His eyes and features grew hard. "Blundertail, there is something I have to tell you."

Andrew suddenly felt chilled. He realized what Ned was going to do. "No, Ned—wait!"

"Why? So you can do this in your own *gentle* way?" Ned asked. "The truth must be told."

"You don't understand."

"I think I do," Ned said. He trembled with emotion. "Blundertail, there were no earthquakes. There were no strong winds. It was you. You turned the signs. And back in Sparklebrook, that was a performance of a very important play that we stumbled into and ruined for people who had been planning it for a very long time."

"No earthquakes?" Blundertail asked meekly.

"On the road that first night, when the carriage approached and Andrew fell, that happened because you knocked him down."

"He might have been trampled by the carriage masters!" Blundertail said.

"I know," Ned said.

The elderly knight stumbled away, shaking his head. "I know you would never lie to me. I know that everything you've said must be true. How could I be so unaware? So clumsy?"

Blundertail hung his head. "I'm such a fool."

One of the Tenontosaurus sauntered up to the small group. He gestured toward Blundertail. "You are a Knight of the Unrivaled, aren't you?"

"No," said Blundertail.

"But your armor, your heroic deeds! Why, if not for you—"

Blundertail raised a single gauntleted hand to silence the other dinosaur. "Yes. If *not* for *me*."

"What modesty and humility," the Tenontosaurus said. "We hail from Diploville. It's not far. Would you accompany us? It would be a great honor."

"I will accompany you," Blundertail said. "But please do not think that I bring any honor or glory with me. I do not. I am a scroll-keeper. A simple scroll-keeper, nothing more."

"Well, that, too, is a noble profession," said the Tenontosaurus. "We have a school. You should visit it. The library is vast."

"Is it?" Blundertail asked, his eyes wide, his claws touching. "I would so like to be near the scrolls again."

"Come, you and your friends are welcome," said the Tenontosaurus. "And if you truly wish it, we'll say nothing but that the signs were turned. A new way will be found to mark the path."

"A sound idea," Blundertail said. "But whatever you do, don't ask me for advice. Ask a great thinker."

Ned followed the dispirited Blundertail.

Lian rested her hand on Andrew's back. "There's more to this, isn't there? You didn't want Ned to tell him."

Andrew looked down and saw the shining breastplate, which had been trampled and banged out of shape. He picked it up.

"There is more to this," Andrew said. "And now I have to figure out how to make things right."

CHAPTER 15

The road leading to Diploville was backed up for miles. Andrew and the others trailed behind a long line of competitors from the race.

"I wonder what's going on ahead," Andrew said. "Maybe someone's in trouble and needs help!"

Blundertail lowered his head. "Then they would do well to avoid me. I have disgraced myself. I have disgraced all the Knights of the Unrivaled."

The wizened Troodon gestured at his armor. "And this armor, once worn by *true* Knights of the Unrivaled, should not be worn by me. If I could reach all the clasps, I would take it off piece by piece, here and now!"

The saurian looked back at Ned. "Be my squire one last time and remove this burden from me. Please."

Ned could not meet Blundertail's gaze.

Andrew looked to Lian. "Blundertail, I'm sure you know the wise words of Idlecrest: 'A misty morning does not signify a cloudy day.'"

"I have no training as a knight," Blundertail said. "I am unworthy of the honor. It was my desire to live an adventure and my pride in believing that I might do so without disgracing myself that has led me to this sorry state."

"I read something else by Idlecrest," Lian said firmly. "'If you are all wrapped up in yourself, you are overdressed.' Put simply, if someone is in trouble and in need of aid, you needn't be a brave knight to try your best to help."

"Yes," Blundertail said, his mood lifting. "I suppose you're right."

Andrew smiled. A light that had been dimming in Ned's eyes leaped back to full flame.

"The three of you should go ahead and see what's happening," Blundertail said. "I'll wait for you in the library."

Andrew groaned inwardly. He had seen something in Blundertail: the makings of a fine and true knight.

But he didn't know what story he could spin that would ever make the saurian believe it.

"Ah, Ned, before you go?" Blundertail asked, tapping at his armor.

Andrew took Ned's arm and led him away. "Time enough for that later. If anyone's in trouble, we'd best not keep them waiting!"

"Of course," Blundertail said. "There is time enough and more."

Andrew, Ned, and Lian left Blundertail and quickly found the friendly Tenontosaurus who had led the blue team in the race.

"The great knight Blundertail the Mighty has asked that we scout ahead for him to see if his help may be needed," Andrew said quickly. "He'd come with us, but the sight of a Knight of the Unrivaled being led through this crowd might cause concern. Best to avoid that, if possible."

"Ah, your knight is wise *and* modest," the Tenontosaurus said. He slipped a ring from his finger and dropped it into Andrew's waiting hands. It was very heavy. "This is a ring of passage. Use it to go where you will."

They navigated through the crowd, showing the ring to all. Many bowed.

"I don't understand," Ned said. "What did he mean about Blundertail being modest?"

Andrew told Ned the story of how Blundertail had used his breastplate to warn the approaching dinosaurs of their peril. He did *not* mention how he continually had led Blundertail to the signs because of his own curiosity. Ned and Lian accepted the information calmly. For some reason, it didn't seem to change things for either of them.

"Don't you get it?" Andrew asked as they made their way through the crowd. "Blundertail can be a great knight!"

"'Reach beyond your grasp,'" Ned said. "'Your

goals should be grand enough to get the best of you.'"

"The words of Idlecrest!" Andrew exclaimed. "Yes, exactly that!"

Ned nodded slowly. "I've known all along that he could make his dream a reality. You were the one determined to make his reality a dream. And now that's done."

Andrew was about to say something else when Lian squeezed his hand. "Give it some time. Give *him* some time. What he did wasn't easy for him."

Andrew said nothing else as they pushed ahead. But he decided that he would not give up on Blundertail. He would find some way to help the Troodon.

All the roads of Diploville were wide enough to accommodate the long-necked Diplodocus who were the town's founders. The tall, ornate buildings had arched doorways and ceilings high enough to admit mighty saurians. Every road was packed, every archway filled. It was chaos.

"What's causing all this?" Ned asked.

Then, at the center of town, they saw a single dinosaur standing at an intersection and doing the worst job imaginable of directing traffic. It was a long-armed Microvenator, who moved with herky-jerky motions, more like a windup toy than a true saurian.

Ned gasped at the sight.

"What's wrong?" Lian asked.

"That doesn't just look like a clockwork dinosaur," Ned said. "It is one! Just like in some of the designs I had in our room!" Ned's trembling hand went to his face. "Blundertail said he had sent copies of my designs to Nallab in Waterfall City. But he never said anything about anyone building one of them. And now look!"

Confused saurians pressed together from all sides.

"What can we do?" Andrew asked. "There are probably clockworks like this at every intersection in the city."

Ned shook his head. "It was a simple design. It should have worked."

"I see a device for winding on the contraption's back," Lian said. "It may have been overwound. It certainly looks that way."

Andrew nodded. The clockwork dinosaur was motioning for one group of saurians to come forward, then another, and still another. It halted one of the first groups, brought out a fourth group, halted another—it was out of control, and nothing was being achieved.

"Can you get close enough to disable it?" Andrew asked.

Lian grinned. "I was fast enough and agile enough even before I trained as a Knight of the Unrivaled. I may have laid down my sword, but I still have my edge."

Before she could dart forward, a voice called from somewhere in the crowd, "Make way! Make way for a Knight of the Unrivaled!"

"It must be Blundertail!" Andrew said excitedly. "He's come after all!"

The crowd parted—and Stonesnout appeared. Clad in gleaming armor, he trotted up to the clockwork dinosaur with a huge net in his hands. Tossing the net, he yanked the contraption off its feet and pulled the net taut. Then he hauled it away.

"I'll have the others cleared away soon!" Stonesnout called.

Cheers rose up, and an Ovinutrix took the mechanism's place, singing a calming song as she helped to clear the streets a little at a time.

"My inventions don't help anyone," Ned said grimly. He turned to Andrew. "Well, now you've gotten everything you wanted."

Andrew shook his head. "I don't understand."

"Admit it. You didn't come on this adventure to help us," Ned said. "You didn't come to see us succeed. You came to see us fail."

"That's ridiculous."

"No. You wanted to be proved right. If the goblet isn't where the scroll said it is, then your point is made. The scroll is just a story, all the scrolls in that room contain stories, and you could be the one to deliver them to Dinotopia. What you don't see is that it would still be about you and not about the stories. Talltail was right about you."

Andrew's chest rose and fell. "Please. Don't think that."

"Why not? It's true." Ned shuddered. "And you wanted to see me fail, too. Well, now you have."

"No," Andrew said. "Please, Ned. You're my brother."

All three spun around as a pair of young boys were thrust into the town square by a disappointed Massospondylus.

"Do you see what you have done?" the dinosaur asked.

"We were just curious," the first lad said. He was eight years old, with curly black hair and wide blue eyes.

"We wanted to see if they could do their job faster if they were wound a little tighter," the second lad added. He had spiky blond hair and he looked about nine years old.

"Now you've seen," the dinosaur said. "Honestly, I don't know how I'll ever teach either of you anything!"

Lian looked at the boys and smiled. One of them waved. Then they were led away.

A bobbing figure rushed up to the trio. It was Storklebeak!

"Where is Sir Blundertail?" Storklebeak asked. "I must apologize to him!"

Andrew was surprised. "Storklebeak, I must apologize to you. I—"

The saurian cut him off. "If I had known that I had Blundertail the Mighty in my midst, I never would have left him on the side of the road. You, young squire, were a chore. But this great knight, the one who brought harmony to Sparklebrook at the time of their greatest need—ah!"

"Harmony?" Andrew asked. "But they had worked so hard on that play!"

"Too hard," Storklebeak said. "They had to learn a hard lesson—that sometimes the thing you most fear is the best thing that could happen. When their production ground to a halt, they were able to see how foolishly they had been acting. They decided to celebrate harmony by acting in concert with one another, by *being* harmonious. Blundertail's wise intervention allowed this!"

"That's wonderful," Andrew said.

"And his latest achievement—why, the city founders are already speaking of chiseling a plaque in his honor," Storklebeak said. "Those signs were dangerous. The least little thing could move them. If not for Sir Blundertail, who knows how many might have been hurt! Jonathan is looking for him. Will you three help?"

Lian grinned at Andrew and Ned. "I think you two should go. I'll be at the Academy of Harmony, in case he's there."

She slipped silently into the crowd before Andrew could ask her to wait. He turned to Ned and Storklebeak.

"Let's find Blundertail," Andrew said. "I think Storklebeak has a tale he should hear."

CHAPTER 16

Lian was quite impressed by the Academy of Harmony. The academy was devoted to the advanced study of saurian and human history and culture. And Diploville was not far from Cornucopia, where the Dinosaur Olympics were held, and where another school was set up to teach humans how to live in harmony with dinosaurs.

She didn't expect Blundertail to be here. She had come for another reason entirely.

After wandering the marble halls for a few minutes, she encountered a guide who took her to the classroom of the Massospondylus—and the two young explorers who had created such havoc in the town square.

The door opened, and Lian's guide, a young woman about her age with straw-colored hair and brown eyes, approached the Massospondylus. Class was in session, and the pair Lian had seen in the street were there.

Good.

"Mistress Amberspots always welcomes visitors," the Massospondylus said.

Lian's young guide bowed her head and left the small classroom. The students were a mixed bunch from the very young to those in their teenage years. Some were human, others saurian. Lian could guess why the two explorers had been admitted to this school. They had an interest in learning. An overwhelming interest. But they lacked boundaries. Lian had been like that once. She had learned the discipline of the sword, the code of the Bushido. But that was not what these two needed. With one simple lesson, the same one she had learned at their age, she was confident that they would be able to channel their energies usefully.

With the teacher's permission, Lian introduced herself to the class.

"You were at Halcyon!" a student cried happily. "With Andrew and Ned Lawton!"

Lian smiled. "That's true. But that's not the story I've come here to tell."

She hauled a satchel over her shoulder. "How many of you believe in magic?"

The students eyed one another warily. Only two hands went up without hesitation.

The two explorers.

"Then I'll focus my attention on you two. What are your names?"

"I'm Leopold," the black-haired lad said. He pointed at his partner. "This is my friend Rollie."

"What's in the bag?" Rollie asked.

"I'll get to that," Lian said. She couldn't restrain her smile. She had the same sense of anticipation that she might feel just before a great joust. "So you believe in magic?"

"We believe that not everything is explained," Leopold said.

Rollie nodded eagerly. "And lots of people call the stuff that's not explained magic."

Lian dropped her heavy travel bag on the teacher's desk. "I suppose you consider transmutation a form of magic."

"Changing lead into gold?" Rollie asked.

"In an instant? With a word or a gesture?" Leopold asked eagerly.

"Changing any one thing into another," Lian said. "People change. Circumstances change. That can be a form of transmutation, too."

Lian glanced at the Massospondylus. She appeared amused and gestured for Lian to continue. Lian noticed that all the other students were listening intently, though they possessed the discipline to wait and see what point Lian would make.

"Is that what's in the bag?" Rollie asked. "Lead to be changed into gold?"

"No," Lian said. "That would be common. And if my sense of everyone in this class is correct, then you are all, to some extent, like me. And you are not satisfied with the common and ordinary."

There was a brief murmur of assent. Mistress Amberspots rapped the wall, and the students settled down into silence.

"I am on a great quest with a Knight of the Unrivaled," Lian said. "We travel to the Valley of Whispers, across from Deep Lake. Because it is there that the members of the Explorers Club hid the Goblet of Gismore, according to an ancient scroll that the knight with whom I travel has discovered."

"Is it Stonesnout?" Rollie asked.

Leopold nodded swiftly. "Yes, he visited us this morning, before, ah—"

"Before you became curious about the clockwork crossing guards?" Lian offered.

Sheepishly, they bowed their heads.

"There's nothing wrong with curiosity," Lian said. "So long as it's tempered with wisdom and patience."

She tapped her bag. "This satchel contains the heart's desire of anyone who possesses it."

A gasp of awe rose from the students. Again Mistress Amberspots rapped for quiet.

"But there is a secret to it," Lian continued. "A secret wisdom that must be applied to make it work. You see, if this bag is taken to the hiding place of the Goblet of Gismore and opened in the presence of the goblet, its true contents will be revealed. If it is opened any sooner, then all you will see is what one would expect to see in any traveler's bag. Some food. Some water. Other essentials. Nothing out of the ordinary. And that's all you will ever find. Unless patience is employed."

Rollie and Leopold were spellbound.

She walked to the middle row of the class and set her bag on the desk they shared. "I'm willing to entrust this bag to you two until I leave. If you can manage *not* to open it and peer inside, I will tell you the answer to a great question."

"What question?" Rollie asked.

Lian laughed. This was just like sparring with a worthy opponent! How joyful!

"I know not only the location of the stone keep of the Great Dragon of the Outer Dark, but also where the dragon is now," Lian said. "You know of the dragon, don't you?"

"We've heard the story," Leopold said.

"This is more than just a story," Lian said. She held out her hand. "Do we have an agreement?"

The two lads hesitated.

"How will you know that we haven't opened the satchel?" Rollie asked.

"I use a form of magic that is all my own," Lian said. "But talking about it would rob it of its power."

Slowly, each lad shook her hand. Lian left the classroom, feeling utterly triumphant!

CHAPTER 17

Ned had searched the streets and the library. He could find no sign of Blundertail. Night was falling, and a thick fog was rolling in. Thunder roared in the distance, and heat lightning streaked across the sky.

He met up with Andrew, whom he barely looked at.

"How could a Knight of the Unrivaled disappear so completely?" Ned asked.

They stood on the steps of a great coliseum.

Footsteps sounded behind them, along with the telltale clanking of armor. Ned and Andrew turned, hope rising in their hearts.

Stonesnout stepped down to greet them. "A true Knight of the Unrivaled could do so easily. The mystery to me is how Wizenscales accomplished the task."

"It's not right that you call him that," Andrew said. "I heard you that day. I know that your plan was to make a joke out of Blundertail."

"He was already—"

Andrew was determined not to let the knight finish. "I know of the seven knightly virtues. The First Code. So does Ned. What you planned was a disgrace to both."

Stonesnout trembled with fury, then somehow calmed himself. "I never meant for him to be dubbed a knight."

"I know," Andrew said.

Ned watched the exchange, startled. He glared at the knight. "Why are you here?"

"An elderly saurian is missing," Stonesnout said. "Finding him before he can come to harm, especially on a night like tonight, is the duty of a Knight of the Unrivaled."

"Then consider yourself released from your duty," Ned said. "We don't want your help."

"Nor am I offering it," Stonesnout said. "I simply told you what I plan to do. The best thing for all concerned is for you to stay out of my way while I bring that old fool in from the cold."

Stonesnout stormed past them. He stopped at the foot of the steps, sniffed, and walked south.

"He has Blundertail's scent," Andrew said.

Ned nodded.

They rose and followed the knight as he walked to the end of town and through a series of fields. Neither spoke. As they walked, the fog thickened. If not for the occasional glint of moonlight off Stonesnout's armor and the metallic clanks he made while walking, they might have lost him completely.

The fields gave way to hills and valleys. Huge stone outcroppings turned the path ahead of them into a maze.

Ned realized the truth first. "We've lost him. I can't hear Stonesnout. I can't see him."

"It's worse than that," Andrew said. "We're lost."

A sudden tap on each of their shoulders made them jump. They turned to see Stonesnout standing before them, holding one claw to his mouth for silence. He angled his head toward the outer edge of a great rock and moved swiftly and silently toward it despite his armor's weight. Andrew and Ned followed.

Beyond the rock lay a great valley. The rising wind carried a powerful, low, steady growl and a pair of voices toward them. Ned saw two figures in the distance—and an object that was as great and tall as any dragon, its wings moving with a slow, powerful majesty.

Andrew shuddered as he felt the chill breeze from the creature's slowly, steadily flapping wings. The mist parted as he strained to see the thing in the distance better, revealing the bold straight lines of its spine and chest, and the craggy misshapen contours of its huge and outthrust head, which was bathed and framed in moonlight. The creature's scent came to Andrew, a strong musk that made him think of things that were at once very old yet powerful and dangerous. And its low, heavy roar rose and fell with its movements, almost like laughter.

The pair standing before the creature were Blundertail and Storklebeak. Storklebeak trembled, but Blundertail held his ground, his chin raised defiantly against his unknowable opponent. Andrew wanted to go to his friend—but his fear had him riveted to the spot!

"It is the Great Dragon of the Outer Dark!" Storklebeak cried.

"It is the unknown," Blundertail replied.

"We have traveled to the Outer Dark," Storklebeak said. "Sir Blundertail, will you protect me? I fear the dragon!"

"As do I," Blundertail said.

"But you are a Knight of the Unrivaled!" Storklebeak said. "Courage, strength, resoluteness—these are among your knightly virtues."

"As is complete honesty," Blundertail said. "I said I feared the dragon. I did not say I wouldn't face it."

Near the tall rock, Andrew shivered and turned to Ned and Stonesnout. He was afraid, but he knew that he could not allow Blundertail to face the dragon alone. "We have to help them!"

"We must," Ned said, surging forward.

Stonesnout blocked his way and muffled a tiny laugh. "Can't you see?" Stonesnout whispered. "It's a bellows, that's all."

Andrew stopped and peered more closely at the dragon. The mist parted once more, and this time, the creature's shape re-formed into that of an old, moaning, creaking machine.

"Those are the dragon's great wings!" Stonesnout said. "The wind is making them move."

Ned's shoulders slumped as he peered ahead once more.

"What an old fool," Stonesnout said with a laugh.

"And what if your eyesight were not so sharp?" Ned asked. "What if you traveled with someone who was afraid and wanted only your protection? What then?"

Stonesnout's mirth quickly faded. "You're right, of course. For the sake of Wizenscales' companion, we should put an end to this."

Andrew's hand shot out and clamped down on the knight's shoulder. "No!"

Ned and Stonesnout stared at Andrew in wonder.

"Let him face the dragon," Andrew said. "We all have to, sooner or later."

"But it's not a dragon," Ned said. "There is no such thing."

"There is in our hearts," Andrew said. "There is a dragon for all of us. Even Stonesnout."

The knight's nostrils flared. "What are you saying?"

"It's your fear," Andrew said. "Growing old. No longer being fit and strong. Being capable of making mistakes. Blundertail embodies that fear. It's why you ridicule him. It's why you wanted him banished. And it's why you're here."

"He should never have been made a knight," Stonesnout said. "Lord Botolf—"

"Lord Botolf made his decision," Andrew said. "And who are we to question it?"

Ned stared at his brother, then turned back toward Blundertail, Storklebeak, and the "dragon."

Blundertail strode up to the bellows. He raised his chin and stared for a good long time. Then he laughed.

"There is no dragon here," Blundertail said. "Come and look."

Storklebeak slowly walked up beside Blundertail. "It's a machine of old. Its growls and roars are just the creaking of its laboring and ill-kept parts."

"Ah, if only Ned were here," Blundertail said. "He has a genius for this sort of thing. He could fix it so that it no longer frightens any poor travelers."

Ned stepped forward. "I am here," he called. Then he rushed to the elderly Troodon and embraced him.

"You weren't going to leave without me, were you?" Ned asked. "I'm your squire. Where you go, I follow."

Blundertail looked past Ned at Andrew and Stonesnout, who also were approaching.

"There are many truths, are there not?" Blundertail asked.

"Yes," Andrew said. "And all stories are true. In some fashion or another."

Stonesnout did not meet the elderly knight's gaze.

"It seems I did not make such a botch of things as I might have," Blundertail said. "But I must be more careful—and I must have complete honesty from my friends. It is one of the seven virtues, after all."

Andrew nodded. He looked ready to say something, but hesitated when a running figure cut across the land and raced their way.

It was Lian, and she was nearly out of breath.

"Leopold and Rollie have run away," Lian said. "They left a scroll behind to say that they are explorers, as in the tale I told them today. They're going to the Valley of Whispers."

"Where the goblet is hidden," Blundertail said.

"Yes," Lian said. "But a storm is coming—a bad one. If the waters of Deep Lake overflow, the Valley of Whispers will be first to flood. We have to find them. We must go now!"

CHAPTER 18

Andrew, Lian, Ned, Blundertail, and Stonesnout traveled in Storklebeak's wagon. The heady aroma of their cargo made it impossible for Stonesnout to scent the missing boys. Besides, the resourceful lads might have caught a ride on one of the fast-moving carriages crossing the island. All the small group could do was attempt to reach the valley first. Fortunately, Braveback knew a shortcut. He always did.

The rains came quickly, a raging torrent that beat upon the sides of the wagon like a constant volley of angry fists. The sky at dawn looked much the same as it had at midnight. By midday, they neared the Valley of Whispers.

Storklebeak kept them entertained, and this time Andrew truly listened to the saurian's tales. He was able to appreciate the sheer joy and excitement that infused Storklebeak as he spoke. The Syntarsus knew how to hold an audience, and he made no secret of how he achieved the task: When Storklebeak told a tale, it was clear that he wanted to hear how things would turn out as much as anyone!

Only Stonesnout did not listen. The words of Andrew's mentor came to him: *There are two kinds of people. Those who listen and those who wait to talk. A storyteller must be an expert at listening.*

Seeing the strong knight sitting in the corner, staring away in displeasure, Andrew felt he could see how he must have appeared the other night.

"I wish I had seen you standing your ground before those rushing herds of saurians," Ned said to Blundertail. "And I'm sorry for what I said."

"Don't be," Blundertail said. "Honesty is one of the knightly virtues. Never apologize for it."

Andrew thought about that. He had not been completely honest. He wanted to tell Ned that he had led Blundertail to those signs, knowing what might happen, but he didn't want to say the words in front of Stonesnout. The knight still half-respected Andrew—and Andrew didn't want to give that up if he could help it.

Stonesnout pushed open a wooden window and gazed outside as a rush of rainwater spattered him.

"It won't be long now," Stonesnout said as he shut the window. "When we reach the valley, *I* will look for the lads who have run off. All of you are filled with wild and foolish thoughts."

Lian tensed.

Stonesnout fixed her with his gaze. "In fact, if not

for your fanciful tale, these lads would not be in danger."

Lian looked away.

"How interesting," Storklebeak said.

"What?" growled Stonesnout.

"I was just thinking about all the knightly virtues. I thought that compassion, mercy, and belief in others were listed among them. I suppose I was wrong."

"You forget absolute honesty," Stonesnout said. "Honesty overrides all other concerns."

"Ah—but honesty relies on truth," Storklebeak said. "And truth is sometimes open to interpretation. One being's truth is another's favorite fantasy. I think you have more than your share of truths that can go in either direction."

A sudden splash and a rocking of the wagon sent everyone but Stonesnout tumbling. He had been holding on to a small metal hook.

"I think I mentioned that we were almost there," Stonesnout said. "That was a true thing, at least from my point of view."

Andrew wobbled to his feet and reached a window. Shoving it open, he saw that Braveback had hauled them onto a road by Deep Lake that was flooded by the rains. Storklebeak pressed close and peeked through the window with him.

"Don't worry," Storklebeak said. "Braveback knows what he's doing!"

"It will be time for me to depart in a few moments," Stonesnout said. "The rest of you may do as you like. Search for your goblet if you wish. Just don't make more work for me by getting yourselves in trouble. I have two rescues to perform as it is!"

Ned leaned back and crossed his arms. "Tell me something, Stonesnout."

The knight looked his way.

"Are you planning to go out there like *that?*" Ned asked.

Stonesnout wrinkled his brow in confusion. "Like what?"

"In your armor," Ned said. "I may be filled with foolish thoughts, but it occurs to me that your armor weighs you down. It may rust, and mud and silt and who knows what else may get caught in its nooks and chinks."

Blundertail leaped up. "Good thinking!"

The rocking of the wagon toppled him again. Ned helped Blundertail take off his armor.

Stonesnout reluctantly shifted his gaze in Andrew's direction. "All right, then. You may assist me."

"I don't think I'm worthy of the honor," Andrew said.

Lian shrugged. "Me neither."

Finally, silent Jonathan helped Stonesnout out of his bright, clean armor.

"Now, isn't that interesting," Ned said. "With both of you out of your armor, I don't think anyone could tell at a glance which of you is the experienced knight and which of you spends most of his time around scrolls."

Blundertail sighed. "Ned, about what I did during the race. There is something you should know."

"Ah, good," Stonesnout said. "More confessions of your bumbling, Wizenscales?"

Andrew wondered if Blundertail was going to tell them all that he had been near those signs only because of Andrew's curiosity.

Suddenly, a loud crash sounded, and the wagon tilted. Everyone slid to the left-hand side of the living quarters, and the wagon stopped moving forward.

"Braveback!" Storklebeak yelled. He and Jonathan thrust open the door and leaped into the floodwater. Andrew hung on to the doors as the winds tore at them. He saw that Braveback was sunk up to mid-flank in the floodwater. Storklebeak and Jonathan were swimming toward him. The wagon was stuck fast.

High riverbanks rose on either side of them. Far ahead, where the waters were much deeper, there was a small island. Several dozen humans and saurians were stranded on it, along with a handful of smashed wagons.

"That was some kind of convoy," Andrew said.

Stonesnout sidled up beside him. "The Valley of Whispers has a small harbor for ships crossing Deep Lake."

"They must have been waiting here for passage

when the rains began," Andrew said.

Stonesnout looked stricken. In a low voice, he said, "In the time we have, it is surely our duty to do as much good as we can for as many as we can help."

Andrew stared at him. "What are you saying?"

"That I can't be in two places at once," Stonesnout said. "I can't search for those lads and still help those on the rise."

Stonesnout squeezed his eyes shut. "A knight must not travel alone. That is part of the First Code. But my pride was such that I never have followed it, and my *luck,* until this moment, has allowed me to do so without consequences. But that has changed now."

Andrew couldn't believe what Stonesnout was saying. He didn't consider Blundertail and the rest of them to be of any use in this crisis.

What did Stonesnout think he could accomplish on his own, anyway? He was right. His pride was his undoing.

Andrew was determined it would not be his. He turned to face Blundertail, Ned, and Lian.

"Blundertail, you only went near those signs because of me," Andrew said. "I knew that you were hitting the posts and spinning the signs with your tail, but I didn't care. I just wanted to know what the signs meant. If anyone had been hurt in the race, it would have been my fault, not yours."

Blundertail shook his head. "But why?"

"I thought they might lead me to a great tale," Andrew said. "One that audiences would want to hear more than the story of my time in Halcyon."

"But you've touched so many lives with that tale," Blundertail said. "Inspired so many people. I've seen them. So has Ned."

"You inspired me," Ned said.

"And Ned was right," Andrew continued. "I didn't want to see you succeed in your quest. I wanted the scrolls to be made-up stories. And I wanted to be the one to bring them to Dinotopia. But that wouldn't have solved my problem. It still would have been about the teller of the tale, not the tale itself."

Andrew saw a tear in the corner of Lian's eye. But she smiled approvingly.

"I don't know if I can be the kind of storyteller I want to be," Andrew said. "But I can try to be the kind of person I want to be. And that starts here. Right now."

Andrew looked at Stonesnout. "You can go on your own, or you can accept our help. But you can't expect us to do nothing in a crisis like this."

Stonesnout hesitated, then said, "What do you think you can do?"

Andrew turned to Ned, Blundertail, and Lian. "I can ask my friends for help. The question is, will they give it?"

First Ned, then Lian, and finally Blundertail came forward.

"What can we do?" Ned asked.

They looked outside.

"The river's rising," Andrew said. "That island will be covered, and the current will be too strong for those who can swim to reach the banks. Most who do get there won't be able to climb to safety. And Leopold and Rollie are out there somewhere. As for what to do—"

Andrew smiled. "I was hoping my brother, the inventor, might have an idea."

Ned paced for a few moments, then peered at the group of humans and saurians on the nearby island.

"I can think of something," Ned said. "But it's a crazy idea. There might be flaws in it. Things might go wrong."

"We have to try," Blundertail said. He placed one claw on Ned's shoulder. "And if something goes wrong, we'll be together to deal with it."

Ned nodded slowly and outlined his plan.

CHAPTER 19

Lian and Stonesnout swam to the riverbank. Fighting the raging tide had nearly drowned Lian. She sank to the ground, water dripping from her clothes and hair.

Stonesnout shook himself. "Invigorating!"

"If you say so," Lian muttered. She was already scanning the cliff side, looking for any trace of Rollie and Leopold.

Stonesnout raised his chin imperiously and sniffed. "Nothing. What makes you so certain they came to this side and not the other?"

Lian stood. She pointed at the cliffs. "Caves, caves, and more caves."

She turned and pointed at the cliffs across from them. "No caves."

"Even if you're right, they could be miles off in any direction," Stonesnout said.

"Listen, just because we're probably going to fail doesn't mean we have to be pessimistic," Lian said.

Despite himself, Stonesnout laughed. "You have

the soul of a knight. Why don't you accept it?"

"I laid down my sword," Lian said. "Where I come from, it had a far different meaning. I can't walk that path again."

Stonesnout pointed ahead. "Let's walk this one, then."

They searched for carriage tracks but found none.

"It's possible that we reached the valley before them," Stonesnout said. He looked uneasily toward the island in the distance. "Or that they're already there."

"They're here," Lian said. "I'm not sure how I know that—I just do."

"You rely on instinct," Stonesnout said.

"It's more than that," Lian said. She kept watch on the cliff side as the rain clawed at her and the buffeting wind at her back shoved her like a giant invisible hand. "Something's not as it should be. I'm looking at it, but I can't quite see it."

"You can't see what?" Stonesnout asked.

"If I knew, I'd tell you."

Stonesnout snorted. "If you had the training of a knight, there would be no mysteries for you."

"Really?" Lian asked. "Then why can't you see it?"

"Because there is nothing to see," Stonesnout said. "There is no movement in any of the caves. And there is no sign that anyone has been here. No tracks in the earth, no climbing gear, nothing. In fact, I've never seen an area look so tidy."

Lian's eyes opened wide. "That's it! They knew they'd be followed, so they've covered their tracks. Only they've covered them *so well* that it looks like no one has been through this area in ages. And we know this is well-traveled ground."

Stonesnout blinked. Several times. "You're right."

Lian grinned and shielded her eyes from the rain. "I bet if we search for the cleanest, tidiest cave up there, the one that looks like no human or saurian has been there in eons—"

"That's where we'll find them," Stonesnout finished.

"I think so," Lian said.

In less than an hour, they had found the cave they were after. The river now flowed over its banks, but Lian and Stonesnout were too busy climbing to notice.

Ten minutes later, they reached the mouth of the cave. A frantic scurrying echoed from within.

"Leopold?" Lian called. "Rollie?"

Silence. Had she imagined the sounds?

"I can scent them now," Stonesnout said. "All we have to do is round them up and take them back."

Lian looked down at the rushing flood. "You're forgetting something."

"I don't think so."

"You're forgetting how difficult it was to get up here," Lian said. "Getting back down will be even more difficult. Especially with unwilling company."

Stonesnout shook his head. "I suppose we could just toss them over the edge."

"Tell me you're kidding."

"A knight is trained to think practically," Stonesnout replied.

"Then that's another reason I'm glad I didn't become a knight." Lian felt a sudden wind at her back. She nearly lost her balance. Then Stonesnout was at her side, shoving her deep into the cave.

"The lads are here," Stonesnout said. "They're safe. We should tend to the others."

"We may never find them again," Lian said. "They'll have realized their mistake, and they won't make it again."

"They have friends, family," Stonesnout said. "I'm sure they wouldn't want to make them worry."

"They're dolphinbacks," Lian said. "They feel like they've only got each other."

Stonesnout sniffed the air once more. "This cavern leads back to a maze of tunnels. We could be here all day. I won't risk the lives of those below on this foolishness."

Lian wondered if Stonesnout was right. She asked, "Have you ever heard the phrase 'An aim in life is the only fortune worth finding'?"

"I have."

"I thought, just for a moment, that I had found my place in that classroom," Lian said. "I wanted to see things grow. It's why I took to the land. But as challenging as farming is, it wasn't the *right* kind of challenge for me. I need the joust, the battle of wills and wits that comes from facing a worthy opponent. That's what I felt in the classroom."

Stonesnout nodded. "Tell me again what you promised them."

Lian recounted the story she had told. The saurian knight pressed deeper into the cavern. "Lads! I am the one who can exchange that bag's contents for your heart's desire. Lian is here, but she is not upset. She has been given her heart's desire already, though she didn't know it. Now come forward, or I will leave, and your opportunity will go with me!"

"What are you doing?" Lian hissed. "They're too smart to fall for trickery. And they deserve better."

"You planned to trick them," Stonesnout said. "The only possible true location of the keep holding the Great Dragon of the Outer Dark is one's imagination. Isn't that right?"

Lian nodded slowly.

"Besides, what I plan is no trick."

They waited patiently for several moments, until a small voice drifted out of the darkness.

"You sure you're not mad?"

It was Rollie.

"Come forward and accept your charge," Stonesnout said.

Rollie stepped into the dim light flowing from the mouth of the cave. Lightning crackled, revealing

143

Leopold a few paces behind him. Rollie held out the satchel. Stonesnout took it from him.

"We didn't open it," Leopold said.

"Good," Lian said. She looked into their eyes and sensed that they were telling the truth.

"What is it you wish most?" Stonesnout asked.

"To know if our families are well," Rollie said.

Leopold shook his head excitedly. "To know if they think of us, if they miss us. We miss them."

"Do you believe that they love you?" Stonesnout asked.

Rollie and Leopold exchanged curious stares.

"Yes," Rollie said. "But—"

"Then you already have your answer," Stonesnout said. "If they love you, then they think of you. And they miss you. If they love you, then they know you would want them to be happy. And if they know that, then they are happy. Because you are with them, even as they are with you."

Rollie and Leopold walked past Lian to the mouth of the cave. She turned and helped steady them against the rushing wind.

Both lads were smiling.

Lian looked back at Stonesnout, whose grim features had softened.

But only a little.

"What's happening down there?" Rollie asked. He pointed at the island.

"Curious?" Lian asked, feeling as if she had taught these lads something. They were finally displaying patience and restraint. Perhaps she *had* found her calling. "Why don't we go down and find out?"

CHAPTER 20

Andrew and Ned helped Jonathan and Storklebeak free Braveback from the harness that had trapped him. Then the group allowed the flood tide to carry them to the island. The waters were rough and frightening, but they soon reached solid land.

The humans and saurians gathered on the island and huddled fearfully. The rains were growing worse, and the floodwater was consuming the shore around them at a steady pace.

Ned explained that they were with the Knights of the Unrivaled and told them exactly how they planned to help. "Here in the deep water, there is no chance to swim for shore. The current is too strong. But we can all make it through this if we work in harmony."

Ned directed the largest of the saurians to gather facing inward in a circle. Braveback helped to position his fellow longnecks so they were all standing side by side, with their bodies pressed as close together as possible.

Then it was time for the humans and the smaller dinosaurs to get to work. As the water smashed the trapped wagon, huge chunks of wood broke loose and floated toward the island. The wood was gathered up, along with all the branches and vines that Ned and the others could find.

"We're going to build a platform that we can stand on. It will be raised up above the floodwater," Ned explained. "It's got to be strong enough to support us all."

As the shore slowly receded, the workers put their fears aside and united. Branches were tied together and long pieces of wood from the wagon were set in place. Harnesses were made for the longnecks to wear.

Lian, Stonesnout, Rollie, and Leopold arrived and helped out.

When the operation was finished, a large platform sat in the center of the island. Vines led from the platform to the harnesses worn by the longnecks. Ned had engineered a series of makeshift pulleys so that the loosely hanging lines could be yanked taut, raising the platform. Looming over them, however, was the chance that the platform could break in half beneath the weight of its burden.

"We're going to use the rising water to help support the platform," Ned said.

As the water smashed into the backs of the sauropods, little cries of fear escaped many of those gathered.

"It's up to you, now," Ned said.

Andrew stood before his audience. He told the tale of Snicknik and the travelers, holding their attention as he held his own with his love of the tale.

As he spoke, the water rose up around the great sauropods. Blundertail, Ned, and Lian went to the most frightened of the dinosaurs, calming them with gentle touches. The rush of the floodwater was deafening, and Andrew had to talk so loudly that his throat soon ached.

Ned paid close attention to the water level. He used nods and gestures to instruct the humans and small saurians on the platform when to tighten the ropes and raise the platform.

Some water washed over the surface, but it quickly drained off as the platform was raised and supported by the water below it.

Andrew watched his audience carefully. He knew the danger they faced. If even one of the sauropods panicked and broke formation, the platform could be pulled apart and they could all be swept away by the flood.

But the longer he told the tale, and the more involved it became, the less he thought of that danger. The rain beat at him and the wind shoved him back and forth, but he flowed with the elements, making it seem as if his every movement was intentional.

"The earth trembled and burst apart as the newly awakened dragon sprang from his keep," Andrew said.

"Gerard stared at it in confusion. He knew the earth. Never had he dreamed that such a creature could come from within it, or that the beautiful songs he sang could bring forth something so frightening!"

"What did the dragon look like?" asked one of the struggling longnecks.

"It was different for everyone," Andrew said. "Some, like young Terrance, saw it and believed it was as vast and unconquerable as eternity. Others, like Snicknik, saw only a beast to be faced and driven off. For Gerard, it had wings of fire and a face that glowed not with anger, but with loneliness and longing. The same longing he had seen his brother facing for so very long."

"What did Snicknik do?" asked Braveback. The water hit him hard and he grunted with exertion—but he kept still.

"Snicknik waited," Andrew said. "His feet itched and his body trembled with desire to do battle. His shield was ready, his sword and his lance. But he held his ground and waited as the dragon circled over—"

Suddenly, one of the great sauropods hollered with pain and surprise as a stone struck his back. He stumbled forward and back, breaking the line that secured him to the already wavering platform. The platform tipped and people screamed. Ned lunged and grabbed a child before she could slide off one end.

"Everyone, we must raise the platform!" Ned shouted. A shower of floodwater mixed with stones and other debris burst onto the platform from its lower edge, raining down with the power to smash anything that lay in its path. Stones tore through the platform and water jetted up through the holes.

Stonesnout turned just in time to see the water reach for him. Then another powerful force smashed against him from the side, and he was knocked out of the way. He rolled and sprang to his feet only to see Blundertail pounded and battered by the water and the rocky cargo it held.

"No!" Stonesnout yelled.

"Work together," Ned hollered. "We have to raise the platform!"

The sauropod who had stumbled now found his footing and rooted himself in place.

Every other human and saurian standing on the shaky platform pulled at the vines, trying to right their wobbling creation, but the water rushed over its surface, quickly covering it in several feet of icy rushing water.

Andrew had to fight to keep himself from being hauled off the platform. He saw a man skid across its surface and slam into a longneck, whose harness he used to anchor himself.

Andrew yelled, "The dragon can be beaten. Anything can be faced. We are what and where we are because we first imagined it! Imagine that we are safe and then make it so!"

The humans and saurians worked in harmony and

soon the platform had been lifted high enough to haul it out of the grasp of the floodwater. The wobbling stopped and everyone looked around with relief.

Stonesnout stood over Blundertail's crumpled, still form.

"He's breathing," Stonesnout said. "Sir—Sir Blundertail is breathing. He will be well. And he will be honored."

Ned looked up at the rain slanting from the sky. Then he looked down and shuddered as the sound of cracking wood rose into the air and the platform buckled.

"There is a flaw," Ned said. "I see it now. There is a flaw!"

The platform wasn't stable. And the constant strain of the vines yanking at it from every corner and points in between would soon rip it to pieces!

Stonesnout called for silence. Blundertail's maw was moving. His eyes flickered, then closed. But his chest continued to rise and fall with his shallow breaths.

"Believe," Stonesnout said to Ned. "It was meant for you. *Believe.*"

"I believe," Andrew said. "If there's a flaw, you can fix it."

In the silence, Andrew heard the rain pelting the water that was now up to his waist. Then he knew.

Ned looked at his brother. Then he lifted his head—and laughed.

"Come together!" Ned called. "All of you, high above, move together and brace the platform!"

The huge sauropods moved inward, the platform pressing against the base of their necks. They had to move carefully, their heads crisscrossing above, casting even more shadows upon the group.

The platform stopped groaning. It rocked, but not much.

They were safe.

"It's so dark," Rollie said.

"Like the Outer Dark," Leopold added.

"This is not the Outer Dark," Andrew said. "It's only shelter from the storm."

Andrew knew that Sky Galleys would be coming soon, along with boats and rafts. Word had been sent from Diploville. But right now he had a story to tell. A story that was far more important than the story-teller.

"The Great Dragon of the Outer Dark looked down at Terrance," Andrew said. "It spoke to him. 'Your brother's beautiful voice called me from my slumber. But your sadness keeps me here. Why are you sad? Do you need wings to fly? You may have mine. Ask for whatever your heart desires, and I will give it to you and take away your sadness.'"

"Did he take the dragon's wings?" Stonesnout asked. He raised his chin. "I could see why he might. To fly above his troubles."

"No," Andrew said. "He looked to Snicknik and

asked what he should do. Snicknik was a Knight of the Unrivaled and a member of the Explorers Club. He was thought to have great wisdom."

"But he was just Feet," Lian said.

"Clever Feet," Ned added.

"Yes," Andrew said. "Very clever feet. He told Terrance that he must choose. Terrance didn't know what to say. He didn't know what he wanted. He didn't know his place in the world."

"But he wanted to find out," Stonesnout said.

"He did," Andrew said. "He said he would be willing to travel all of Dinotopia to gain the answer. He would explore every mystery. To seek and to find—that was what he wanted."

"He was an explorer!" Leopold said.

"And he didn't realize it," Rollie added.

"Snicknik held out his hand to Terrance and asked him if he would like to travel with the Explorers Club," Andrew said. "Terrance looked at his brother and all the members of his family, who said that they would miss him, but that they cared more for his happiness than for anything else in the world."

"What about the dragon?" Stonesnout asked.

"The dragon wanted only to return home," Andrew said. "But he had forgotten the way. Gerard recalled a song that he often sung when he had strayed from his path. He sang it until the dawn arrived and the dragon had disappeared."

"And that's how it ends?" Lian asked.

"That's how *that* story ends," Andrew said. "But there are always others."

"Then tell us another," Storklebeak said. "Tell us one of a land where the sun always shines!"

Andrew smiled. "I will."

"How can it always be bright?" Stonesnout asked. "There must always be darkness. Always night to go along with day."

"In the place I'm thinking about, the brightness of the sun burns in the hearts of everyone who lives there," Andrew said. "So even if there is darkness or rain, there is always sunshine and brightness, too."

"It sounds like a dream," Ned said.

"No, it's very real," Andrew said. "Because in this place, a person can learn that there is more to life than building things, especially when he has already built something that is strong and long-lasting. Like the friendship you share with Blundertail. I think that's what the valiant knight was trying to say. Just believing in one person can be of more value than you ever might have expected, and such a thing can affect untold lives."

"Where is this place?" Lian asked.

"Haven't you guessed?" Andrew asked. "It is the most wonderful place I know. It is called Dinotopia."

EPILOGUE

Andrew sat in Blundertail's library, helping the anti-quarian organize his newly discovered scrolls. It wasn't the easiest task in the world. Stonesnout was always around, for he had developed a love for scrolls second only to that of Sir Blundertail, the First Knight of the Scrolls.

Ned continued to invent things, and Blundertail encouraged him.

"Things don't turn up in this world until some-body turns them up," Blundertail said.

One night, when Andrew and Blundertail were alone, the elderly saurian said he had a confession to make.

"That day, during the race? Everything I did came out of a story," Blundertail said. "I'd read of a knight facing a similar trouble, so I acted as he acted."

"That only makes what you did more impressive," Andrew said. "You acted on faith that what you read in a scroll would work in the real world."

"You really think so?" Blundertail asked. "You really think I acted bravely?"

"I know you did," Andrew said. "'Make the most of all that comes and the least of all that goes.'"

"Idlecrest's words!" Blundertail said. He sighed. "I've been told that after we were rescued, the waters rose so high that the entire valley was flooded. If the Goblet of Gismore was hidden in those caves, it may be lost forever now."

"It wasn't needed," Andrew said. "The greatest bringer of harmony I've ever known was there at a time when he was needed the most. A goblet is just a goblet. But your spirit saved us all."

Blundertail patted Andrew gently on the back. "You're a good lad."

"I have a confession, too," Andrew said. "I'm returning to Talltail. I plan to visit Lian in Diploville, where she's learning the art of teaching. But I don't know how long it will be before I come back this way again."

"But I've had no time to copy these scrolls," Blundertail said. "How will you take these stories to your mentor?"

"I don't think it's my place to do that," Andrew said. "You discovered them. You believe in them. As the First Knight of the Scrolls, the honor and glory of telling the tales on these pages should go to you."

"Who will look after my library when I'm traveling?" Blundertail asked.

A mild snore sounded from a resting couch nearby. Stonesnout lay curled up with a scroll near his claws.

Andrew and Blundertail laughed, and quietly made their plans for a bright and happy future.

ABOUT THE AUTHOR

SCOTT CIENCIN is a best-selling author of adult and children's fiction. Praised by *Science Fiction Review* as "one of today's finest fantasy writers" and listed in *The Encyclopedia of Fantasy*, Scott has written over thirty works, many published by Warner, Avon, and TSR. For Random House Children's Publishing, Scott has been a favorite author in the popular *Dinotopia* series, for which he's written four other titles: *Windchaser*, *Lost City*, *Thunder Falls*, and *Sky Dance*.

"I grew up with a love of the fantastic," says Scott. "Being given the opportunity to write novels set in the world of James Gurney's Dinotopia put me on a path of discovery...In creating Dinotopia, James Gurney became the heir to the legacy of Jules Verne and other classic fantasists. Having the opportunity to add to the mythology he's created has not only made me a better writer, it's taught me lessons about the limitless vistas of the imagination."

Among Scott's other recent projects is the children's series *Dinoverse,* a six-book fantasy adventure that takes readers on an exciting and humorous journey through the Age of Dinosaurs. Scott's *Dinoverse* titles include: *I Was a Teenage T. Rex* (#1), *The Teens Time Forgot* (#2), *Raptor Without a Cause* (#3), *Please Don't Eat the Teacher!* (#4), *Beverly Hills Brontosaurus* (#5), and *Dinosaurs Ate My Homework* (#6).

A WORD FROM DINOTOPIA® CREATOR JAMES GURNEY

Dinotopia began as a series of large oil paintings of lost cities. One showed a city built in the heart of a waterfall. Another depicted a parade of people and dinosaurs in a Roman-style street. It occurred to me that all these cities could exist on one island. So I sketched a map, came up with a name, and began to develop the story of a father and son shipwrecked on the shores of that island. *Dinotopia,* which I wrote and illustrated, was published in 1992.

The surprise for me was how many readers embraced the vision of a land where humans lived peacefully alongside intelligent dinosaurs. Many of those readers spontaneously wrote music, performed dances, and even made tree house models out of gingerbread.

A sandbox is much more fun if you share it with others. With that in mind, I invited a few highly respected authors to join me in exploring Dinotopia. The mandate for them was to embellish the known parts of the world before heading off on their own to discover new characters and new places. Working closely with them has been a great inspiration to me. I hope you, too, will enjoy the journey.

James Gurney

Look for these other Dinotopia titles...

WINDCHASER
by Scott Ciencin

During a mutiny on a prison ship, two very different boys are tossed overboard—and stranded together on the island of Dinotopia. Raymond is the kindhearted son of the ship's surgeon. He immediately takes to this strange new world of dinosaurs and befriends a wounded Skybax named Windchaser. Hugh, on the other hand, is a sly London pickpocket who swears he'll never fit into this paradise.

While Raymond helps Windchaser improve his shaky flying, Hugh hatches a sinister plan. Soon all three are forced into a dangerous adventure that will test both their courage and their friendship.

RIVER QUEST
by John Vornholt

Magnolia and Paddlefoot are the youngest pairing of human and dinosaur ever to be made Habitat Partners. Their first mission is to discover what has made the Polongo River dry up, and then—an even more difficult task—they must restore it to its usual greatness. Otherwise, Waterfall City, which is powered by energy from the river, is doomed.

Along the way, Magnolia and Paddlefoot meet Birch, a farmer's son, and his Triceratops buddy, Rogo, who insist on joining the quest. Together, the unlikely foursome must battle the elements, and sometimes each other, as they undertake a quest that seems nearly impossible.

HATCHLING
by Midori Snyder

Janet is thrilled when she is made an apprentice at the Hatchery, the place where dinosaur eggs are cared for. But the first time she has to watch over the eggs at night, she falls asleep. When she wakes up, one of the precious dinosaur eggs has a crack in it—a crack that could prove fatal to the baby dinosaur within.

Afraid of what people will think, Janet runs away, hoping to find a place where no one knows of her mistake. Instead, she finds Kranog, a wounded Hadrosaurus. Kranog is trying to return to the abandoned city of her birth to lay her egg, but she can't do it without Janet's help. Now Janet will have to face her fears about both the journey ahead and herself.

LOST CITY
by Scott Ciencin

In search of adventure, thirteen-year-old Andrew convinces his friends Lian and Ned to explore the forbidden Lost City of Dinotopia. But the last thing they expect to discover is a group of meat-eating Troodons!

For centuries, this lost tribe of dinosaurs has lived secretly in the crumbling city. Now Andrew and his friends are trapped. They must talk the tribe into joining the rest of Dinotopia. Otherwise, the Troodons may try to protect their secrets by making Andrew, Ned, and Lian citizens of the Lost City…for good!

SABERTOOTH MOUNTAIN
by John Vornholt

For years, sabertooth tigers have lived in the Forbidden Mountains, apart from humans and dinosaurs alike. Now an avalanche has blocked their way to their source of food, and the sabertooths are divided over what to do. The only hope for a peaceful solution lies with Redstripe, a sabertooth leader, and Cai, a thirteen-year-old boy. This unlikely pair embarks on a treacherous journey out of the mountains. But they are only a few steps ahead of a human-hating sabertooth and his hungry followers—in a race that could change Dinotopia forever.

THUNDER FALLS
by Scott Ciencin

Steelgaze, a wise old dinosaur, has grown frustrated with his two young charges, Joseph and Fleetfeet. They turn everything into a contest! So Steelgaze sends them out together on a quest for a hidden prize. But someone has stolen the prize, and the two must track the thief across the rugged terrain of Dinotopia. Unfortunately, their constant competition makes progress nearly impossible. It's not until they help a shipwrecked girl named Teegan that they see the value of cooperating—and just in time, because now they must face the dangerous rapids of Waterfall City's Thunder Falls!

FIRESTORM
by Gene DeWeese

All of Dinotopia is in an uproar. Something is killing off *Arctium longevus,* the special plant that grants Dinotopians long life—sometimes over two hundred years! As desperate citizens set fires to keep the blight under control, Olivia and Albert, along with their dinosaur partners, Hightop and Thunderfoot, race to find a solution. But Olivia is secretly determined to claim all the glory for herself. In her hurried search for answers, what important questions is she forgetting to ask?

THE MAZE
by Peter David

Long ago, a raptor named Odon left Dinotopia's society to live in a dangerous maze beneath the island. Despite their fears, Jason, Gwen, and a witty young saurian named Booj are determined to reach Odon. Gwen's father is suffering from a deadly disease, and Odon, once Dinotopia's wisest healer, is their last hope for a cure. Will the three friends make it through the Maze? And even if they do, how will they ever convince the mysterious hermit to help them?

RESCUE PARTY
by Mark A. Garland

Loro is a young boy who dreams of adventure. He wants to travel, while his stepsister Ria is happy keeping up with everyone in their hometown of Bonabba. The problem is that Ria and their Styracosaurus friend, Trentor, can hardly keep up with Loro.

When a deadly storm hits Bonabba, the three friends witness a hot-air balloon heading toward the Rainy Basin. Trentor is worried about his father, a Basin trail guide, and Loro wants to follow the balloon. Soon Loro's dream comes true as he and his friends embark on a mission to rescue and explore. But are they walking into danger?

SKY DANCE
by Scott Ciencin

Ever since he was small, Marc has wanted to be a tightrope walker—even though he has no sense of balance and a fear of heights. His buddy Gentle, a Parasaurolophus, dreams of being a musician—even though his notes are wildly out of tune. Through sheer determination, the two join a troupe of traveling entertainers. They learn quickly, but their newfound skills are put to the test when tragedy strikes. A Sky Galley flies out of control during a terrible storm. Only an aerialist like Marc can save the passengers. But performing isn't easy when lives are on the line!

CHOMPER

by Donald F. Glut

Exploring near the Rainy Basin, thirteen-year-old Perry and his Montanoceratops friend Stoutpoint come across an unusual find—a hatchling Giganotosaurus! Unable to resist the baby's cries of hunger, Perry and Stoutpoint rescue the injured dinosaur and take him back to their village. There, Chomper conforms to a harmless diet of fish and invertebrates, proving that humans and meat-eaters *can* peacefully coexist! But when the dinosaur's appetite outgrows the village stores, something has to be done. Does Perry have the courage necessary to return Chomper to the dangerous jungles of the Rainy Basin?

Some Favorite
Dinotopian Expressions

"To have strong scales" = to be tough, to have thick skin

"To roll out of the nest" = to leave the island

"To crack through the shell" = to pass into adolescence

"A rolled-up scroll" = someone whose behavior is puzzling or unpredictable

"Something is boiling in the pot." = Something is about to happen.

"To look at someone from horn to tail" = to look someone up and down

"To be in the horsetails" = to be lost or overwhelmed

"To be in someone's scroll" = to be in good with someone

"Sing and it will go away." = Take your mind off your troubles.

"Jolly-head" = someone amusing

"Head-scratcher" = worry, problem

"Breathe deep, seek peace." = Take it easy, peace be with you, farewell.